MIRRORS AND MIRAGES

Also by Monia Mazigh

Hope and Despair: My Struggle to Free My Husband, Maher Arar

MIRRORS AND MIRAGES

A Novel

MONIA MAZIGH

TRANSLATED BY FRED A. REED

ARACHNIDE

This edition published in 2014 by
House of Anansi Press Inc.
110 Spadina Avenue, Suite 801
Toronto, ON, M5V 2K4
Tel. 416-363-4343
Fax 416-363-1017
www.houseofanansi.com

Distributed in Canada by
HarperCollins Canada Ltd.
1995 Markham Road
Scarborough, ON, M1B 5M8
Toll free tel. 1-800-387-0117

House of Anansi Press is committed to protecting our natural environment. As part of our efforts, the interior of this book is printed on paper that contains 100% post-consumer recycled fibres, is acid-free, and is processed chlorine-free.

18 17 16 15 14   1 2 3 4 5

Library and Archives Canada Cataloguing in Publication
Mazigh, Monia
[Miroirs et mirages. English]
Mirrors and mirages / author: Monia Mazigh ; translator: Fred A. Reed.

Translation of: Miroirs et mirages.
Issued in print and electronic formats.
ISBN 978-1-77089-359-7 (pbk.).—ISBN 978-1-77089-360-3 (html)
I. Reed, Fred A., 1939–, translator II. Title. III. Title: Miroirs et mirages. English.

PS8626.A96M5713 2014   C843'.6   C2013-907016-8
                              C2013-907017-6

Cover design: Marijke Friesen
Text design and typesetting: Alysia Shewchuk

 Canada Council Conseil des Arts
for the Arts du Canada   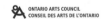 ONTARIO ARTS COUNCIL
                                CONSEIL DES ARTS DE L'ONTARIO

We acknowledge for their financial support of our publishing program the Canada Council for the Arts, the Ontario Arts Council, and the Government of Canada through the Canada Book Fund. We acknowledge the financial support of the Government of Canada, through the National Translation Program for Book Publishing, for our translation activities.

Printed and bound in Canada

MIX
Paper from
responsible sources
FSC® C016245

MIRRORS AND MIRAGES

_1_

Emma felt her heart beating, steadily at first, then faster and faster. It was as if her chest were going to burst. What had come over her? Was it excitement or fear? She slowed down and then stopped in front of a dark red door. It belonged to a brick house, one of a row of five small dwellings hunched together, the wood trim around their tiny windows stripped bare by weather and time. The door of her future home bore a visible mark at its centre, like a claw scratch on the weather-worn wood.

She shivered. From where Emma stood, she could see the backyards of another, identical row of houses, and through a moss-splotched wooden fence, clumps of soil that must have been part of a garden. The fence planks, rotted by the damp and encrusted with dirt, had been torn away or had fallen. In one of the backyards, the residents had seeded small plants. Their yellow flowers lent a festive air to the grim decor, while the greenish yellow weeds reminded her of a small park long untended. In one of the weed-choked gardens Emma thought she could make out a rusty metal cage, its door hanging from one hinge; the animal it housed had fled, never to return.

She could feel her eyes being drawn once more to the door of her new home. She noticed the grey beneath the peeling red paint. Just beside the door there was a high, narrow window. *Must be the kitchen*, she thought. Emma stood on tiptoe, but she was too short to see over the windowsill.

The exhaust fumes from the cars and buses that rushed along the busy street had stained the dark brown brick so it looked almost black. The row houses were all two storeys: a ground floor and a second floor. Mustering her courage, Emma looked up. Directly above the front door she saw another window, and above it, crooked grey asphalt shingles overlapping like fish scales. Suddenly she felt a light, repetitive tug on her skirt. Turning, she saw a slender little girl whose hair, which was pulled back into pigtails, made her look like a frightened rabbit. The girl was no more than seven or eight years old, and in her thin arms she held a pudgy, curly-haired baby whose eyes sparkled with mischief.

"Are you looking for someone, lady?" asked the little girl with the pigtails.

Emma was startled, at a loss for words. Her first impulse was to say nothing. But the girl's insistent look and the smile on the baby's lips changed her mind. She forced herself to smile and said, "No, I'm not looking for anyone. I'm here to see number seventeen. I'll be moving here in a few days."

The little girl seemed relieved. With a shift of the hip she lifted the baby into a more comfortable carrying position and answered calmly, "Well, then, we'll be neighbours." And as suddenly as she had appeared she turned her back and hurried off, still carrying the baby. Emma watched her until she went into one of the neighbouring houses.

Her mind wandered for a moment, and then she remembered why she had come. She knew the neighbourhood; she had seen it many times before when she used to take her daughter, Sara, to school. She didn't care much for the area — it reminded her of her native Tunisia. Images of poverty made her feel queasy. She remembered those grey days when she had walked along this very street. The sight of garbage bags and abandoned furniture had only added to her depression. Once she had seen a derelict fridge, door ajar, amid the piles of rubbish. Refuse littered the sidewalk, waiting for the big green truck to collect and grind it in its cavernous belly. She had never dreamed that she would live here one day. Her life had turned upside down; her childhood dreams had evaporated; she was alone with the past, and it haunted her every day. The perfectly behaved little girl, the brilliant student, the curious young woman, and the courageous immigrant in a new world — all of that belonged to the past. A shadow seeking only to hide, to flee from the judgement of people around her and the constant battering of regret.

Emma glanced at her watch. It was almost noon. She walked back to the bus stop. The bus shelter wasn't far from her future home. Pieces of broken glass lay scattered across the sidewalk, and old circus posters hung in tatters from the lampposts. She paused for a moment to try to make out the odd word that remained.

For the past three months she'd been staying at a women's shelter with Sara, counting the days until she could get out. The sight of the blue metal bedstead was enough to make her stomach churn when she woke up in the morning. She hated the shelter because it reminded her every day of her failed career, of her failed marriage, of her tormented life. But she had no choice: for all her aversion, for all her loathing, her fears, and her demons, the shelter had been the only place to open its arms and take her in.

Now, today, she could permit herself to hope, even to dream of returning to the warmth of a home she could call hers. A letter had come a few days before, informing her that her application for subsidized housing had been accepted. She held tight to that letter for fear of losing it, and to reassure her: soon things would be better.

Last night—it must have been after midnight—she had awakened with a start. Ideas were racing through her mind. She got up and tiptoed to the bathroom, not wanting to turn on the light, as Sara was sleeping peacefully. There, in that cramped space that smelled of cheap perfume and urine overlaid with bleach, she stood in front of the mirror, her nightdress touching the washbasin. She switched on the light and reread the letter. Then she closed her eyes, and for the first time in months a smile brightened her face.

Seated in the shelter waiting for the bus, she slowly opened her bag and reread the letter—that fabulous letter!—for what must have been the nth time. Yes, she and her daughter would have a place of their own. And she had seen it with her own eyes; she was not dreaming, it was real. She listened to herself breathe. She was coming back to life…

2

Louise looked in the mirror once more. She didn't recognize the person staring back. The blue-and-white veil covering her chestnut hair made her look like a nun. One of those austere, remote members of the religious order her mother had so often told her about when she described her unhappy childhood in Chicoutimi.

Without her hair framing it, her face reminded her of a plump, shiny apple. The red cheeks that had always embarrassed her — it was as though she was always blushing — were tightly enclosed by the scarf wrapped around her head. Her blue eyes didn't have the same sparkle that had made her former classmate Big Jean burst out with childish delight, "Your eyes are the same colour as Lake Memphremagog!" She'd blushed that day, but deep down she was pleased. She remembered his innocent compliment. But today, in front of the mirror, she found herself almost repulsive. She forced a smile, but when she looked at her reflection even her mouth startled her. It seemed so small, nearly invisible. With the headscarf on it was as though she could no longer speak: her thin lips were even more compressed. "I can't do it, I can't go out wearing this headscarf. I look awful…" With a quick gesture she took it off. Her fine hair, which she'd pulled up into a bun, stood on end from the static effect of the scarf. She looked at the square of fabric, smoothed it with her slender hand. 100% POLYESTER. MADE IN CHINA, she read along the edge.

She'd bought it the day before at the Bay in the Rideau Centre, not far from the University of Ottawa. The saleslady had shown her different ways to wear it: around her neck like a tie, or thrown over her shoulders, with a large knot at the chest. Louise had smiled politely but said nothing. Did she dare say that the scarf would be covering her hair? Could she face the world with her new self, her new face? Still smiling, she paid the cashier and went home.

A dart of guilt shot through her mind. Hadn't she just become a Muslim? Hadn't she pronounced the *shahada* at the mosque in front of all the women? Some of them had had tears in their eyes, and others ululated with joy. So why was she afraid to cover her hair, to face the world, to testify to her faith? Was it fear of rejection? Of what her university professors and friends who didn't know she had become a Muslim would think?

Then her mother's face came to mind: serious, livid. Their last conversation rang in Louise's ears. "How could you dare sink into the darkness of a religion of people from the desert, people who want to invade us with their incomprehensible ideas, their backward values, their flocks of women and babies?" her mother had lashed out at her. "Listen to me, Louise! I was brought up in the Catholic faith, and the nuns told me exactly what I could and couldn't do; they stuffed my head full of it. I've had it up to here with anything that has to do with religion! I sacrificed my youth for you, I gave you all my love. You're not going to come and start telling *me* about good and evil, about what's sacred and what's religion...So please, do me a favour and get off my case!"

Alice Gendron stood up abruptly from the kitchen table. Her nostrils were flaring, something that happened whenever she lost her temper. Then she rushed off to her bedroom and threw herself down on her bed.

She was a good-looking woman of average height, with short brown hair streaked with grey. She was in her forties and worked as a nurse at the Montfort Hospital. Her team liked and respected her seriousness and her dedication to her patients and her profession. Only two things mattered in her life: her work and her daughter, Louise.

Men hadn't been a part of her world since she was twenty, when Louise's father had walked out on her to pursue his career. That was the year she'd landed with her little checked suitcase on Rue Édouard-Montpetit, primed to enrol at the Université de Montréal.

She had been young and ambitious. Leaving her native Chicoutimi, she settled in Montreal, where she hoped to make a career. Quebec was effervescent with new ideas; the Quiet Revolution had ended, a new era was beginning, and Alice was intoxicated by everything that was happening around her. She could feel change throbbing in her veins. She wanted to fill her lungs with freedom and to forget how miserable her childhood had been. She wanted to bury once and for all the memories that kept popping into her mind—the massive doors of the residential home, the stern faces of the nuns, the smell of cleanliness that assaulted her nostrils like strong perfume, the shiny wooden floors in the main prayer room, but most of all, being removed from her mother and separated from her sisters and brothers.

She met Pierre a few months after arriving in Montreal and registering for her courses. It happened one evening at a friend's house. He was a political science major who dreamed of becoming a lawyer. It was love at first sight. They lived together for two years—two years that almost wiped away the despair and unhappiness of the past. Pierre was from a wealthy Outremont family; the two of them would change Quebec, he promised her. Theirs would be the greatest generation, he told her, over and over. Alice dreamed of freedom and justice. But after he learned she was pregnant, Pierre never set foot in their apartment again. It was over. For him, everything was crystal clear: his career as a lawyer came first; love and babies came far behind.

Alice's deepest fears returned to haunt her. With Pierre her life had meaning; she had believed in him, had learned to believe in humanity once more. And then she'd lost everything. She decided against an abortion, though it would have been easy enough. Montreal was full of clandestine clinics; she could have gotten rid of the being that had turned Pierre against her. But something deep inside held her back. Could it have been the Sunday sermons of her childhood creeping back into her conscience? Had fear of sin caught up with her? Alice Gendron couldn't tell. After weeks of hesitation, of doubt, of tears, her mind was made up. She would keep her baby. Unexpectedly, Louise's birth gave her new hope. Louise became everything: her friend, her daughter, her reason for living.

Louise gave her the determination to continue her studies to become a nurse. It wasn't easy, but Alice had done it. There would be no man in her life. Now, stretched out on her bed, eyes wandering across the ceiling, Alice was furious with Louise, furious with herself for having always given her daughter the right to ask questions, for having brought her up without religious restrictions of any kind.

Her daughter had chosen to become a Muslim. And she — the atheist, the woman who could not tolerate the influence of religion in people's lives — was living under the same roof as a believer who happened to be her own flesh and blood. What kind of trick had fate played? Destiny had turned against her, helped by all that she held dear.

3

Daddy dearest,

Well, I started my courses at the University of Ottawa last week! Here's my course load: microeconomics, macroeconomics, financial math, and statistics! Our profs are flooding us with more info than we can handle, but don't worry. I think I can manage!

In just three years, your darling daughter will be graduating with a bachelor of business administration, meaning she'll be able to give you a hand there in Dubai. I really miss you!

Here at home, nobody understands me. Mommy won't let me stay out after seven o'clock!! I don't think I mentioned that she has a new friend who drops by for a cup of Turkish coffee every morning. Leila is her name, from Lebanon. It won't be long before the Arab League headquarters moves in with us. What an awful woman! The way she looks at me, really nasty, as if I'm some kind of party girl. Maybe she doesn't like my hairdo. Whenever she sees me, she whispers "May Allah help you in this infidel land" over and over.

But you should see the way her eyes are made up, and her Calvin Klein headscarf. What a hypocrite! I just don't understand Mommy. Why does she put up with these women? I guess it's because when Lynne, Mona, and I leave for school, she's bored, so she invites them over to pass the time.

Too bad you're not here with us. How is your work going? Is your partner still insisting on that deal with the Chinese? Just three more years and I'll be able to help you manage the business. I can hardly wait for the time to pass!
Love and kisses,
Your loving daughter,
Lama

Lama laid her pen down on her desk. She got to her feet, stretched, and then folded the letter and slipped it into an envelope.

She wrote regularly to her father, Mr. Ezz Bibi. He had been living in Dubai, in the UAE, for the past several years. The letters were her only escape from the sense of suffocation that came with living in the family home. She looked forward impatiently for classes to begin, for the chance to see her friends, to study, to laugh, to enjoy life the way it was meant to be enjoyed.

Ottawa suited her just fine; she was happy that her parents had decided to immigrate. Unfortunately, her father couldn't stay with her, her mother, and her two sisters. He had remained in Dubai to work and sent them money. If he didn't, who would pay the bills: her and her sisters' tuition fees, their mother's extravagant expenses? She was always changing the furniture, the bed linens, the drapery, then inviting her friends over to display her latest extravagance, drink Turkish coffee, and study the grounds at the bottom of the cup that would predict the future.

Lama hated everything about her mother's hypocritical lifestyle, the way she hid her boredom and the failure of her marriage by parading their wealth in front of her so-called friends. She didn't like it any better that her mother hid behind religion, forbidding her from coming in late while she continued to spend her father's hard-earned money hand over fist, all so they could live a comfortable life in Canada.

Lynne and Mona, her two sisters, didn't share her feelings. They went along with their mother's lifestyle. It didn't bother them. In fact they too loved to shop and to spend money on things they didn't need and didn't even want.

Lama, lost in thought, heard her name. It was her mother calling.

"Laaa-maa, will you come here, please!"

Closing the door behind her, she went down the white marble staircase. An immense chandelier hung from the ceiling above. It lent the entry hall the majestic appearance of a five-star hotel lobby.

The house's first owner had been a bankrupt Italian building contractor. He had built the place himself, using Italian marble; the magnificent kitchen had an imported ceramic tile floor. Its combination of Mediterranean look and luxury had charmed Samia Bibi, Lama's mother. It was the house of her dreams: it reminded her of her childhood in Kuwait, the country her parents had chosen after they fled the war in Palestine and the loss of their ancestral lands.

Samia had always been accustomed to the good life. Her

father was a physician, her mother a teacher. Her family never wanted for anything: they employed Sri Lankan maids, a Filipino cook, and an Indian chauffeur — whatever was necessary to lead a happy, peaceful life. But things hadn't worked out that way for her. Her life was sad and melancholy, as was her elder sister Selma's. Most of the time their parents were caught up in their work while their two daughters spent the afternoon with the servants, watching soap operas on television. So, when Samia first laid eyes on the beautiful house on a quiet crescent in the Ottawa suburbs, her mind was made up: *This is where I'll find my lost childhood, this is where I'll find happiness.*

Ezz Bibi, her husband, wasn't quite so sure. The house was expensive, well above his budget, but he couldn't turn back. Buying the house would mean that he was an investor in Canada. He could establish himself and his family and they could become permanent residents. His wife had cornered him and he couldn't refuse — it was then or never. In a few days the house was theirs.

When Lama entered the kitchen, she could hardly believe her eyes. In the middle of the room stood Samia. Shopping bags lay strewn all over the dining table. Her mother was wearing a short, shiny gold dress, her arms spread wide like a snooty top model, her eyes glistening as if she were a little girl with a new doll. When she saw Lama, she burst out, "How do you like my new dress? Really cool, don't you think?"

Lama was speechless.

"I bought it for Dina's wedding. You know, Suzie's daughter. Ah, I can hardly wait to see the look on Leila's face. She won't believe her eyes when she sees me!"

Lama found her tongue. "But Mother, what are you doing with a dress like the ones girls wear to the clubs? Shouldn't you be wearing something a little more conventional, a little more modest, like you're always telling me to wear?"

In a flash Samia's expression changed from delight to indignation, and then to anger. "So I'm an old lady now, is that it? Maybe I should hide myself? And what's immodest about this dress? Isn't it better-looking than your ratty outfits? Let me remind you that it's a party for ladies only, which means we can dress exactly as we like!"

Lama opened her mouth to reply, but the battle was lost before it began. Her mother was going to wear the dress and it was her daughter's job to encourage her.

She turned on her heel and went up to her room. She had a paper on statistics due in a few days; it was time to get to work. Her sisters would look after complimenting their mother on her purchases. They wouldn't criticize her attempts to look beautiful and modern before the other ladies.

4

It was raining. The drops drummed insistently against the window. Sally was seated in front of her computer, paying no attention to the heavy rain, or to the storm raging outside. A faint smile played across her lips as she read the message Sheikh Abdurrahman Bilal had posted on his website: *It is forbidden for a woman to show her face; many scholars, may their souls rest in peace, are quite clear in this regard: no woman who fears Allah and the Last Day may display her face. If she does so, she will commit an unpardonable sin.*

Sally jumped as the call to prayer sounded from the BlackBerry on her desk. She stood up and hurried off to the bathroom, where she whispered a short prayer, attempting to remember the right words in Arabic, which unfortunately eluded her. Uttering what she could recall, she began to perform her ablutions. Furtively she glanced at herself in the bathroom mirror. How innocent her large black eyes and long eyelashes looked. Her straight black hair, gathered at the neck, made her look severe. As she came out of the bathroom, a few drops of water shone on her slightly protruding forehead. Behind her she had left the sink and the counter splashed with water. No time to wipe up—the prayer couldn't wait. No matter. Her mother, Fawzia, would clean up after her, she was sure.

She returned to her room and spread her little prayer rug on the floor. What a find, that rug of hers! She'd bought it via the Internet; she could fold it up into a small packet and take it with her wherever she went. At one end of the rug was a tiny electronic compass that showed the exact direction of Mecca every time she unrolled it for prayer. She raised her hands level with her head, according to the sheikh's instructions on the website. Self-satisfied, like a pupil getting a high mark, she began to pray.

Sally attended her classes at the University of Ottawa clad in an ankle-length black jellaba, or "jilbab," her face covered by a black scarf that left only her eyes showing. Her mother, who covered her hair with a lightweight scarf, begged her to dress "normally," but Sally wouldn't listen. Her mother had bought her long skirts and handsome, elegantly decorated scarves in place of the black ones she wore, but Sally wouldn't give an inch. Her heart was hardened, and not even her mother's tears could melt it. *Satan is crafty and vicious*, she told herself. *I will resist every effort, everything that leads me to destruction, to lose my soul.*

But there was nothing satanic about Fawzia's actions. She was a believer and had always prided herself on her modesty. Her only wish was that her daughter turn away from this new kind of Islam. She didn't know anything about it, so she ignored the new laws.

When she finished praying, Sally sat down in front of her computer. She was scheduled to participate in an online chat session that was about to begin. The subject: women wearing pants. She'd chosen an attractive pseudonym: Technogirl.

She was proud of her technological accomplishments. She could help her friends choose the right computer and install new programs that made it possible for her to communicate with people around the world. It was a heaven-sent gift, she liked to think. No one could accuse her parents, Ali and Fawzia Hussein, of ever refusing to buy her a device she needed or a computing manual she couldn't do without. In fact they bent over backwards to make Sally happy, always ready to help her succeed in her studies and become a computer programmer, as they had always dreamed. Over the years, all their plans had come to pass. Sally was studious and serious and kept close track of the latest discoveries in the field. She spent hours in front of her computer, read everything she could. It hadn't taken long for her to become an expert.

Sally was the only child of parents born in Pakistan. Her father had a degree in electrical engineering but had never been able to find work in his field. For years after arriving in Canada he tried repeatedly to get a job with a Canadian company in the Ottawa area. But his applications were rarely acknowledged and a handful of interviews led nowhere. It was always the same old refrain: "We're looking for someone with Canadian experience." But how was he supposed to get that experience if no one would give him a chance to show what he could do, to display his abilities?

Ali Hussein had begun to despair. Fawzia, his young wife, had just come to Ottawa to be with him. He could feel the pressure building day by day, pressure to find a decent job and start a family. He couldn't afford to start his studies over again to earn a Canadian degree, and besides, there was no guarantee that he would find work in his field even then. A friend from his hometown who had also immigrated to Ottawa had an idea: they would pool their efforts and become taxi drivers, sharing the car and the profits.

At first Ali Hussein held back; he didn't like the idea at all. He, an engineer, the pride of his family, the ambitious young man who'd come to Canada to build a new life, plunge into the modern world, and improve his economic situation, was going to end up driving a taxi? What would his family in Pakistan think? And his friends? How could he show his face back home? What would be left of his self-respect when people found out he was a taxi driver? He shared his doubts and fears with Fawzia. She was a simple, modest girl from the same small town, and she didn't care what people said. In a loving voice she told him, "There's nothing wrong with working as a taxi driver. This is Canada, not Pakistan. Nobody is going to judge you here. It's honest work — why shouldn't you do it?"

It was the best advice Ali Hussein had ever received. It was as if the *Night of Power* stood revealed before him. From that day on he became a full-time professional taxi driver. In a few years' time he bought his own automobile. He even bought Fawzia a sewing machine. With her nimble fingers she stitched together traditional Pakistani-style tunics and trousers, which she sold to friends and neighbours.

Heaven had smiled on the couple, or so it seemed, except that no children had brightened their home. Finally, seven years after their marriage, Fawzia got pregnant. Sally became part of their lives, and changed those lives forever.

The moment she was born, Ali Hussein vowed to give his daughter every opportunity to succeed in this great and vast country called Canada. He named her Sally, a modern, upbeat name that would help her fit in. His darling daughter wouldn't have to face the obstacles he had had. He wanted her to be able to study, to work. He wanted her to be the engineer he couldn't become. He didn't want her to suffer from discrimination on account of her name or her accent. So it was that Sally — coddled, protected, all but spoiled — took her first steps in the world. Fawzia sewed her the finest clothing: not traditional Pakistani garb but lovely wool, cotton, or velvet dresses with Peter Pan collars and ribbon and lace trimmings.

Today when Sally looked at photos from her childhood, she saw a little girl with smooth jet-black hair worn in pigtails or a bun, looking for all the world like a character from a fairy tale, a perfect model child. Sally attended English-language public school, spoke English, and felt exactly like her schoolmates — except perhaps at Christmas and Easter. Neither Christmas nor Easter was celebrated in the Hussein household. Her parents were Muslims and they made it clear to Sally that she was Muslim. They were observant, prayed regularly, did not eat pork, fasted during Ramadan...but not much more. Still, in their minds they were good Muslims. Sally didn't ask her parents many questions; she did what she was told, but in her little girl's heart she dreamed about Christmas and Easter. No matter how many gifts her parents gave her, she would have loved to receive one from Santa Claus, just like her schoolmates, or join the hunt for chocolate Easter eggs and bite into one.

She had long repented of those inane, infantile ideas. She had found the true path. Allah had rescued her from the dark labyrinth. She wanted nothing to do with modern life and its superficiality. She had found belief—the real, pure belief. And all of it thanks to the Internet, to exceptional websites that seemed to pop up everywhere, speaking of the Muslim faith. What a blessing was technology! This was not the disfigured Islam of her poor parents but the real thing, the religion of the great sheikhs who preached on their sites.

Before finding the straight path she had always wanted to be pretty, polite, and pleasing to her parents, her teachers, and her friends. She had wanted to become a computer programmer with a brilliant career. *A crazy, stupid little infidel* was how she saw herself now, now that she'd gained a new maturity in front of her computer screen, thanks to the learned texts of the Internet's virtual scholars.

5

It was Emma's last day at the women's shelter. The day before she'd picked up some cardboard boxes at the drugstore to pack up the few belongings she'd kept after the breakup of her family.

Her nine-year-old daughter, Sara, was at school. Her parents' painful divorce had hurt her too. Before, she was a happy little girl with a smile on her face, always asking questions. She was like a little bird; her delicate features, her constant chirping, her startling agility, and—above all—her gaiety brought Emma constant delight. But the little bird had suddenly fallen silent, retreating into mute distress.

Emma had met Fadi in Montreal. She was Tunisian, he a Lebanese Canadian. Born in Lebanon, he had immigrated to Canada with his parents at age four. The two met at university—Emma was enrolled in the computer engineering program at the Montreal Polytechnic Institute. She was an outstanding student, at the top of her class. On graduating from high school she had won a scholarship from the Tunisian government, which wanted more women with high-tech degrees to return home one day to work in the public service. The country would be seen as a liberator, an emancipator of Arab and Muslim women.

But politics was the farthest thing from Emma's mind. Honours meant nothing to her; she had no connections with any feminist movement. She only wanted one thing: to be successful in order to support her sick widowed mother. Leaving for Canada had been the hardest, most wrenching decision she'd ever had to take, but her mother, with her gentle and generous nature, had implored her to leave: "Go, my dear daughter. You need to learn about the world, to grow up. We'll meet again some day..."

The first months in Montreal were the worst. Emma's only thought was to give up and return home to Tunis. Every night when she went to bed, she buried her face in her feather pillow and wept. Classes were demanding; everyday life was full of stress; her classmates were cold and remote. And the competition was fierce—everyone wanted to come out on top. The native Quebecers stuck together. Emma couldn't get close to them. It was as if a thick wall of ice separated her world from that of the students with the bright white smiles, the blonde hair, the milky skin.

Emma made friends with girls from diverse backgrounds: Lebanese, Armenian, Vietnamese, Polish. Together they worked on projects. Their courses and programs were a constant subject of discussion, with problems to solve, assignments to prepare. They rarely discussed their private lives.

She lived for her studies, in a room in the university women's residence. Every Sunday she called her mother to hear the latest news from home. It was her only escape from the pressure of classes and from her own isolation. She and her mother chatted about everything.

Zeina, their neighbour's daughter and one of Emma's former schoolmates, had gotten married. The wedding ceremony, the guests' outfits, the pastries—everything was described right down to the tiniest detail. Emma listened with keen interest. "And Zeina's bridal gown, what was it like?" she asked, with a touch of envy.

"Simply magnificent! Embroidered with gold thread, done by girls from Nabeul—the best embroiderers in the country, as you know. And sweets that melted in your mouth, made with pistachios, not the usual almonds. A real wedding, with a real man, from one of the great families of Tunis. I know one of his aunts; she's married to one of my cousins."

There was no stopping her mother as she skipped from one subject to another, pausing for an instant before picking up the thread of her story once more. For an hour, maybe more, Emma was transported back to the warm, heady atmosphere of her native land, swept along by the poetry of the words that her mother must have plucked straight from a fairy tale. And when her mother's rheumatism got the better of her, she would listen as her daughter related what she'd eaten the previous week or described the unbelievable amount of coursework she'd submitted to her professors. No matter the subject of their telephone conversations, Emma looked forward to Sundays, when she could pour out her heart and spin a fresh cocoon that would keep her safe and warm during the week to come.

Through the window Emma watched the passing cars. The bus stopped to take on passengers, then drove off in a cloud of black exhaust fumes. The sky was turning dark, threatening. A storm was coming. Her life in the student residence was far behind her. The cocoon had fallen away and the butterfly had emerged, never to return. How would she cope with her new life, she wondered, without a job, and with a nine-year-old to care for?

The cardboard boxes lay around her, open, half empty. Emma could hardly focus on what she was doing. Memories flooded her mind. She was happy to leave the shelter and move into a place she could call her own. But she feared her new life, feared how others would see her, feared the incessant calls from her mother, pleading for her to return home and try her luck in Tunisia.

The metal bed frame creaked as she stood up. Atop the dresser sat a tiny radio-cassette player that she hadn't yet packed. She pressed the Play button and all at once the melodious sounds of her favourite song filled the room. The hypnotic Arab harmonies pouring from the tiny box contrasted sharply with the dreary space, almost stripped bare of furniture and photographs. Emma walked over to the window as the song lyrics rang in her ears, telling her that all was well, and for an instant she felt happy. Standing there, eyes anxious still, she watched the cars roll by.

Unexpectedly, she felt the urge to dance. Swaying to the rhythm of the music, she moved her hands and arms awkwardly while swivelling her head. The dresser stood in her way, so she shoved it aside. She was no longer in the women's shelter; she had been transported back to Tunisia. She felt young again, and brimming with energy as she skipped like a gazelle across the sands of the Sahara. Then, with a click, the cassette ended.

The song was over. Emma was panting. *What am I doing?* she asked herself ruefully, as though she had not been the young woman swept up in the dance. Her chest rose and fell; her slightly curly hair was dishevelled, strands that had slipped from the bun atop her head floating insouciantly about her face. *I'm not going to let myself get carried away by that silly song,* Emma thought, as if to punish herself for her musical escapade.

She pinned her hair back in place, took a deep breath, tied her bathrobe with a double knot, and turned mechanically back to her cardboard boxes. Only one thing mattered now: she had to get out of this place as soon as she could.

6

The lecture was well under way. For a half-hour Professor Fong had been struggling to explain the principles of financial actualization to the thirty-odd students seated in front of him. At first his accent had given the students the impression that he was speaking Chinese. Eventually they'd adjusted, but the lengthy and laborious calculations that accompanied his examples might just as well have been Mandarin ideograms. When the professor saw the looks of confusion on his students' faces and realized that they were lost, he, who should have shown patience, became irritated instead.

Erasing everything he had written on the blackboard, he began to explain it all over again. "If I gave you the choice between three dollars now and ten dollars in three years, what would you choose?"

The students glanced at one another. Everyone had an opinion. Some giggled; others rolled their eyes, asking themselves why they'd made the mistake of signing up for this particular course. Lama chewed on her pen in consternation. She wanted to answer the question, but had no idea how to go about it.

The hum in the lecture hall had become almost a roar. Professor Fong was losing patience, and in a loud voice he called for silence. Then, taking a deep breath, he began his explanations and mathematical models all over again. A few students let out whoops of delight. At last they'd begun to grasp what he was talking about. Some looked on bewildered, while others glanced at their watches in the hope that the day's lecture would be over soon.

Lama's face lit up. She began to understand as she followed the professor through all the steps, making the same calculations and obtaining the same results. She was a dynamic young woman with a constant smile, a powerful appetite for work, and an even stronger motivation to succeed. She wanted nothing more than to complete her degree in business and join her father in Dubai. Her life with her mother and two sisters weighed on her more heavily each day. Not that she didn't like them, no, but she could no longer put up with the hypocrisy and the superficiality of their relations.

When they'd immigrated to Canada four years ago, Lama had discovered another way of looking at the world. She had been an adolescent then, searching for answers to the questions that welled up within her. Her entire childhood had been spent in Dubai. She'd attended the American school there, along with children from the Emirates and other children of immigrants like her. There were Palestinians, Lebanese, Egyptians, and Americans, not to mention other nationalities. Their parents had come to work in that country, which, ever since the discovery of oil, had become one huge construction site that drew millions who hoped to make their fortunes from the gushing wells. For Arab immigrant families like Lama's, Dubai was heaven on earth. There was work, an Arab Muslim culture, and business was booming, all infused by the aroma of unchained capitalism and the flash of wealth.

Mr. Bibi, Lama's father, had been working like a man possessed for years. His Emirati associate, Mr. al-Arish, a distant cousin of the royal family and a pious man of means, had taken to business the way a fish takes to water. He had all the tools for success: excellent birth, an alliance with the ruling dynasty, money, and a head full of ideas about how to transform his country into an oasis of beauty and economic development in the middle of the desert. Still, as the saying goes, nobody's perfect—Mr. al-Arish didn't speak English. He had attended Qur'an school for a few years and had memorized only a handful of verses before his father's death thrust him into the business world.

Al-Arish had rapidly proved to his paternal uncles and his closest friends that business was second nature to him. He could sniff out opportunities and never seemed to make a mistake. So it was that he located Mr. Bibi, who worked as a consulting accountant in one of the al-Arish Group's companies. Immediately he recognized him as a conscientious, ambitious, professional employee of integrity—but primarily he saw Mr. Bibi as someone who spoke fluent English and who could act as his right hand, opening a door to the outside world for his business.

Mr. Bibi believed it was an opportunity not to be missed, a childhood dream fulfilled. Before long the two men became associates. But he never rested on his laurels, and continued to work as hard as when he had been a simple employee. A cloud hung over his success, however. He was not a native of Dubai, and was always looked upon as an immigrant, a stateless Palestinian, just another among countless foreigners.

The same feelings tormented Lama whenever she came home from school in Dubai. She felt alone, rootless. Always different. Cringing, she recalled a particularly painful incident. Her mother was backing out of the school parking lot to drive Lama and her sisters home. The car scraped the rear-view mirror of a red Mercedes with tinted windows. It was nothing serious, just a scratch. Lama's mother was upset enough with herself, but then a woman wearing huge designer sunglasses leaped out of the other car.

Lama and her sisters looked on in silence. The woman, one foot touching the ground, the other still inside the car, held the door as if to certify that it belonged to her. Sunglasses pushed back atop her head, her posture and expression betrayed her arrogance. She wore a long black robe with glossy embroidered motifs, wayward strands of hair peeked out from under the black shawl that covered her head, and her dark red lipstick matched the Mercedes. Everything about her seemed to shout easy money and vulgarity, and her gestures and body language spoke for themselves. She burst out sarcastically, "So, not only are they foreigners, they're driving cars."

Her face twisted with scorn, she mocked Lama's mother who was clearly not a native of the Emirates, but who lived there and even drove a car. Not only did her country accept foreigners, she insinuated, but they were doing quite nicely, thank you, and even getting rich.

Normally Samia Bibi would never let that kind of remark go by without a reply to match. But this time she held back. Was it because of the children in the back seat? Did the woman's haughty attitude intimidate her? Or was it simply because she was afraid to speak up and defend herself in a country that wasn't her own? She muttered some incomprehensible excuses and then roared off, leaving the woman standing there with a stunned expression on her face.

Lama had been twelve years old. The woman's attitude, and her words, had hit her like a blow to the stomach. She wanted to do something, to defend her mother, but she felt so powerless, so insignificant.

For Lama, immigration to Canada meant the search for a country she could call her own. She wanted to make real friends, build ties with people, and begin to feel at home. Back in the Emirates, everything, from the ostentatious wealth to the superficiality of social life, rang false. Everything, including her relationships with her friends. She felt as though people were watching her every move, scrutinizing her every step, as though she was never appreciated or liked for who she was. Her mother and sisters had fallen into the trap of vanity — her mother because she felt she had to and out of laziness, and her sisters out of imitation and childishness.

Lama's arrival in Canada had transformed her life. At last she could go about her business without having to worry about what people would say. She could make the friends she wanted and she could relieve herself of the heavy, exhausting burden that Arab culture and tradition had become.

7

Ever since she found the true path Sally's life hadn't been the same. She performed her prayers meticulously. She covered her body from head to toe so that not even the slightest hair showed. She covered her face except for her eyes and wore black gloves. But her radical transformation had not kept her away from her computer and from the Internet. She was continually online, reading up on Islam and participating in the multiple forums she found there. In fact, it was when she discovered those forums that Sally had begun to take an interest in her religion.

Up until then, religion had been an accessory for her, something that made her feel good about herself; a kind of talisman that helped her to get what she wanted from her parents, to display the "model daughter" label. Now all of that was behind her. At twenty-one she was brimming with self-assurance. She didn't need fetishes to succeed in life; she wanted nothing to do with traditional Islam of the kind her parents practised. She wanted a pure, unadulterated Islam, an Islam that would make her feel strong and superior. And the only way to do that was to return to the source, to learn the truth about everything.

So it was that the Internet became Sally's saviour, the light in her darkness, the only avenue to the only reliable sources—those of true Islam. For every question that arose, she simply consulted the collections of ready-made *fatwas* available on the Internet. Should she pray while wearing makeup? Should she show her face and hands in public, or should she wear gloves? Should she speak on the telephone in her normal voice or should she place her hand over her mouth when speaking to strange men (wasn't it forbidden to speak to strangers, and wasn't the female voice seductive)? You could find everything you wanted on the Internet. But you had to make sure to visit the right sites—those that promised pure Islam, not those others that claimed to be Muslim but were really agents of corruption that confused young people even more.

Sally's parents, Mr. and Mrs. Hussein, no longer knew how to deal with their only daughter. The earthquake that had destroyed their peaceful family life had caught them unawares. At first they were pleased when their daughter sat down in front of the computer to study and to consult websites—it all seemed normal to them. Sally was an excellent student who had never caused them the slightest concern.

Sally's mother kept sewing fashionable dresses for her, made from the best fabrics to suit the season. But as time passed, Sally began to turn her back on the clothing her mother made for her. At first Fawzia thought her daughter didn't like her creations, that she preferred clothing off the rack. It was Sally's age, she reasoned. "She's still young, and trying to affirm her personality," she concluded, and with her customary simplicity she let things ride.

But Sally only wanted to wear the jilbab. At first she didn't cover her hair, leaving it tied up in a bun at the back of her head. She spoke to her parents less and less. She did not tell them that what she read on the Internet was making her more certain day by day that she must reject their impious life-style and draw closer to God. Gradually she felt resentment towards them creeping into her mind. *Why do they live like infidels? Why doesn't my mother hide her hair in front of strangers?* She did not hate them, but she had begun to call her entire life into question, and with it the principles her parents had handed down to her.

Sally and her family were at odds. For her, every day was like a struggle between good and evil. For her parents, it was like a wound that only seemed to worsen, a wound they had no idea how to heal. Even Fawzia's best efforts and Ali's affec-tionate gaze could not extract Sally from the coldness that enveloped her. What she respected above all were the legal opinions of the sheikhs she followed with such fervour on the Internet. With goosebumps on her skin and tears in her eyes, she would enter a state of euphoria, carried far away from the cares of the world. Strong in her faith, she was prepared to confront the whole world, even her parents.

Sally was stretched out on her bed. An anonymous mes-sage had just popped up on her BlackBerry. Her hands were moist, her heart beating in staccato cadence. It was not just any message—it was a virtual love letter.

The wind is blowing
I shake
Your eyes bewitch me
I turn pale
Take me with you
I'll wait patiently
As beauty awaits her love

A sweet, probing poem, simple and deep, that resonated within her. It was signed *The Boy Next Door*.

Never had words troubled Sally so much. Not even the day when she had decided to wear her long black dress and cover her face, in spite of her mother's abundant tears. On that day she had become mute as a stone, a creature without emotion; she did not even answer her mother. She was on the straight path, of that she was certain.

Mrs. Hussein could not stop crying; she coughed, sniffled, and rubbed her eyes, which had become as red as two fat tomatoes.

"How dare you go out dressed like that?" she shouted at her daughter.

Sally could barely look at her. She felt serene, and the haughty look on her face tore at her mother's heart. "Mommy, you just don't understand what I'm doing. This is how we're supposed to dress. This is the right way."

Mrs. Hussein felt as though she were speaking to a total stranger. She couldn't grasp what Sally was saying. "But back in our village, no one covered their face, not even the imam's wife, and God knows how pious she was."

Sally shrugged. "Those people are fools. They do not read, they don't even have access to the Internet. They've distorted their religion. They don't know the true rules of Islam. Those people ... we'll have to re-Islamize them!"

Sally's mother felt as if a dagger had pierced her heart. She couldn't accept that such hard, such horrible talk could be coming from her daughter's mouth. She walked out of the room with a prayer on her lips, her eyes moist with tears.

Sally was pleased with her performance; she had to tell her mother the truth. She was imperturbable. But as she lay on her bed, the words of the poem swirled in her head, infusing her heart with a rich new perfume, and she was almost trembling. Who in the world might be interested in her?

She had hidden her whole body in order to protect herself from temptation. She had chosen the path of purity and powerfully rejected that of exhibitionism, of disbelief and superficiality. Every day she struggled against her parents' lackadaisical attitude and their ignorance of the true precepts of God by being as strict and intransigent as she could. Who could possibly be interested in her? Moreover, the interested person was a boy.

"O Allah, I beg you to forgive me, forgive me all my sins," she whispered, as though she were terrified of her own thoughts. She was more than certain there was no boy living on their street. And even if there were, she couldn't have cared less. She wasn't going to read such spiritually corrupt messages! Hadn't her sheikh told her that whatever turns human beings away from the adoration of almighty God was illicit, was *haram*? No, there could be no doubt about it. Worse yet, the note was poetry, a form of expression that the *ulema* didn't agree upon. Who knows, maybe she had even committed a sin by reading those verses.

She got to her feet abruptly. The blood drained from her face. She hurried into the bathroom to wash and perform her ablutions. She wanted to purify herself of the filthy words that had crept into her body. By tomorrow she would have forgotten all about that bad joke, she was sure...But in her confusion, Sally forgot to say *insha'Allah*.

God had other plans for her.

8

Nancy Ajram's voice filled the hall: *"Dearest, come close, feast your eyes on me."* The top Arab pop star warbled as a crowd of girls and women undulated in the middle of the dance floor.

This wasn't merely belly dancing but entire bodies moving every which way, back and forth, whirling, bobbing, and weaving. The younger girls lifted up their hair with both hands. With languorous eyes they swung their hips with consummate skill. They shook their shoulders, thrusting forward the daring cleavage of their evening gowns. Their elders, thick of thigh and round of belly, tempered by age and many pregnancies, danced modestly, letting their hands follow the rhythm of the song.

As if on cue, a tight circle formed around Samia. The sequined dress that barely reached her knees looked as if it were painted on her body. She was small, svelte; round after round of dieting and long sessions at the slimming centre had kept her relatively fit, at least in the eyes of most of the ladies who knew her. She danced at the centre of the group, like a squirming earthworm surrounded by hungry beetles. Her limber body swayed from left to right as her eyes, caked with kohl and mascara, darted furtively in all directions.

The other women's gazes dripped jealousy, but their forced smiles, their outbursts of laughter, their clapping, and their flattering banter created a joyous, animated atmosphere. Samia kept on spinning and thrusting her shoulders forward. It was as if she'd been transported back in time, to Kuwait twenty years ago.

SHE WAS STUDYING English then, and she would dance with her girlfriends and dream of a Prince Charming who would carry her away to a wonderful life, far beyond the surrounding desert and the social suffocation of everyday existence. Her choice of English was the first step in drawing closer to the West. She was determined to acquire the tools that would help her break free from this land that was killing her softly day by day. The only thing that gave her the illusion of freedom was the monthly get-togethers at the home of one or another of her girlfriends.

She and her friends would dance, put on extravagant makeup, smoke a few furtive cigarettes, and then sit down to watch an Egyptian tearjerker. For all her escapades, Samia considered herself a good Muslim. She wore a headscarf and prayed, though not always regularly (there were days when she felt too tired or felt her faith a bit weak). Deep down she knew those things were only extravagances, and that she was a good girl at heart.

When she finally found a husband, things would be different. Finding that husband had become her obsession. Her parents wanted her to marry a Palestinian, as her cousins had done. But Samia dreamed of a Lebanese man, an Arab Don Juan who would whisper in her ear with a cultivated accent, who would cover her with diamonds, who would make her laugh — in a word, someone who would bring her happiness. She wanted a well-mannered man, handsome, wealthy, and of a good family. Unfortunately, among all the sons of the Palestinian families they knew, there was no such person. They were ugly, too dark, too skinny, too fat, too serious, too religious, sons of families that weren't as well off as she would like.

THE CIRCLE OF dancing women had expanded. Samia was the star of the evening. Her eyes gleamed, her breath came in gasps as she spun round and round. She hoped she'd succeeded in making all the other guests green with envy. She couldn't be entirely certain, but in the days following this marriage ceremony she would know for sure. The morning get-togethers over steaming freshly brewed Turkish coffee would quickly give her an answer. Tongues would be loosened and the gossip would be flying thick and fast from house to house.

The ceremony was in honour of the wedding of her friend Suzie's daughter to an Egyptian of Palestinian origin. Little Dina, the bride, was perched atop a broad armchair decorated with artificial flowers and pink and purple balloons. She'd had her hair cut in a pageboy and wore a gown specially imported from Dubai for the occasion. Malicious rumours had had Dina just about ready to move in with her boyfriend,

John, a half-Irish Quebecer, but Suzie, in a last-ditch attempt to change her daughter's mind, had introduced her to the son of a friend.

It was love at first sight, exactly who Dina was looking for: a Westernized young man who spoke perfect English, was slightly effeminate, appeared not to be excessively intelligent, and could tell funny stories that made people laugh until they cried.

"At least he's a Muslim," repeated Suzie with a contented air. Then she added, with a burst of laughter, "Poor John — and he's not even circumcised!"

She was proud to have brought Dina back to the straight path, to marry her to a Muslim, not to mention a Palestinian. A divine gift if ever there was one. The first thing she did was call her sister, who was living in Jordan, and ask her to sacrifice a lamb and distribute the meat to the poor. It was a promise she'd made in her prayers, and they had been answered.

Dina never saw John again, and a few months later everything was ready for the marriage. Those weeks and months had been dreamlike. So much had happened in her life in such a short time. She was a new woman. Her fine words to her friends, warning them not to emulate their mothers, evaporated in the heady atmosphere of the approaching wedding. Her criticisms of tradition fell silent. Dina had surrendered to the invisible hand that with every passing day pulled her closer to her mother and to her roots. With a distant look on her face, an uncertain smile on her lips, she greeted the guests who filed past her with a nod. She had lost the battle against her mother and against her own principles, but tonight all she wanted to do was forget her defeat and turn the page. This was a time not for regret but for celebration. Dina stood up, and a handful of older ladies stared with disapproval as she too began to move to the music.

From across the room Lama watched the beautiful people. She knew most of the women would cover their hair and put on long garments that concealed their cleavage before leaving the reception hall. If a touch of makeup remained on their cheeks and eyelids, a hint of lipstick on their mouths, well, that was too bad. It was night, and no man would see them except for the husbands who came to pick them up.

Lama felt terrible about the way her mother was dancing. What a shameful way to behave! How she hated the hypocrisy. And to top it off, she was still in shock that Dina had decided overnight to drop John, her boyfriend, and fling herself into a new adventure. Did Dina really love her new husband? How could she turn her back on someone she loved one day and embrace a lifestyle she'd always despised the next? Dina, hair dyed blonde and dripping with flashy jewellery that the sister and mother of her new husband had draped around her wrists and neck, didn't seem worried in the least by the astonishment, the bedazzlement of the guests.

"What a mess," Lama sighed, over and over. Her mother and two sisters were still dancing. She picked up a morsel of baklava and popped it into her mouth. The aroma of rosewater and the strong taste of honey brought a grimace to her face. She could hardly wait for the party to end.

9

Alice Gendron's hands were shaking. Read the newspaper? Impossible. She could not concentrate. A brief dispatch caught her eye. Despite her agitation, she managed to read it:

> *The ambassador of an Arab country has annulled his marriage after learning that his future spouse, who wore a niqab (full-face veil), had a beard and suffered from strabismus, according to a report published Wednesday in an Emirates newspaper. The ambassador had agreed to wed the resident of a Gulf country on the basis of photos provided by the family, which turned out to be those of the bride's sister, the report added. In the course of his rare meetings with his fiancée, the ambassador had not been able to see her features as she wore a niqab, according to the article. Once the contract had been signed he discovered "when he attempted to kiss his wife, a physician, that she had a beard and suffered from strabismus." He filed a petition with the court, alleging that he had been "duped" by his parents-in-law, and divorce was granted. The source did*

not cite the nationality of the diplomat nor of the wife. Women
in the Gulf monarchies often wear veils when they appear in
public, and some wear the niqab, or full-face veil.

The frail sheet of newsprint quivered in time with Alice Gendron's trembling hands. How she would have liked to freeze them, to hide them, to cause them to vanish for a moment, to forget them, to forget how unhappy she was. Fortunately there were no other nurses in the staff lounge to observe her state of distress.

The microwave, the mini-fridge, the red couch...everything was in order, everything was clean, everything was just as it should be. But the item she'd read was by no means as harmless and banal as Mme Gendron would have found it a year ago, before her daughter became a Muslim. Now her daughter's actions were calling her and her life deeply into question.

Louise had turned her back on her liberty to enter a hermetic world, a closed space where women looked like identical articles for sale. The idea of Louise in a veil made her shudder. She didn't even want to glance at the newspaper. She hoped a hearty laugh and a good breakfast would sweep away her nervousness—at least, that would have been the solution before Louise's life fell over a precipice, dragging her down too. Mme Gendron pushed the newspaper as far from her as she could, as though she hoped to erase from memory what she'd just read.

Alice's world had collapsed. Everything had become strange, abnormal, bizarre. She could not understand what had driven her daughter to choose that path. *It can't be her choice!* Alice insisted, in a final effort to deny reality. *They must have brainwashed her at university, I'm sure of it.* She was furious with herself, with her stupidity and her naivety, but most of all she was furious with Louise. *Why didn't I see it coming? All the to-and-fro, all the so-called conferences with those Arab friends of hers. Wasn't that obvious enough? I should have put my foot down, showed more severity, more foresight. I should have spotted the problem before it got out of hand . . .*

But how would she have gone about it, she who'd always been so open-minded, so confident? It would be against her philosophy of education to stick her nose into her daughter's life. She hadn't brought up her daughter with threats, with the fear of punishment. Above all, she hadn't wanted to treat Louise as she had been treated. She'd always allowed her to express herself, to show her curiosity, to ask questions.

Religion had been absent from Alice's life for years. Her childhood memories, which were dominated by religion, were bitter ones. There were moments of nostalgia when she felt like turning back to the past, when she looked hard for a glimmer of faith, a tiny twig of happiness, but she could find nothing. The pain was too sharp, her resentment too strong. So she closed her eyes and tried to forget, to concentrate on the present. That was her only source of happiness. But today, even that light had begun to flicker, and it threatened to die, extinguished by Louise's capricious behaviour.

In becoming a Muslim, Louise had reintroduced the spectre of a dark past into their household. And she was trying to nurture the flame of faith with another religion, a foreign, terrifying, unknown religion that sent chills down Alice's spine. *How could my daughter have caved in to her friends' pressure?* How could she have agreed to sacrifice her liberty, to lock herself away in an archaic and chauvinistic moral system, one that was underdeveloped and anti-feminist? How could she have thrown over all that had been won after years of struggle for the emancipation of women, and now submit herself body and soul to the grip of a religion that stood for the exact opposite?

What has happened to Louise? Does she really hate me that much? she repeated, over and over.

Just then the door opened and her friend and co-worker Christiane came into the room. They'd been working together for years. Christiane knew almost everything about Alice; they talked over their worries, their everyday problems, their workplace disagreements, and their arguments with the physicians. It didn't take her long to notice how strained Alice's face looked.

"What's the matter? You're white as a sheet. Are you feeling okay?"

Alice could not answer. She would have liked to start sobbing, to let her friend comfort her, but fear held her back, took away her voice. Was it fear of being seen as an unworthy mother, a mother who had failed to train her daughter to discern freedom from illusion? Or was it shame at displaying her vulnerability?

The words came with a rush, only to catch halfway in her throat, blocked by fear. Alice Gendron was a strong woman; she would not let misfortune get the best of her. Louise's metamorphosis would not beat her. She was not about to lower her guard. But deep down inside, for the first time she felt a tiny crack, the smallest fissure. Was mother-love getting the better of her or was she getting older and weaker? Ideas tumbled over one another in her mind. What should she answer? She had no idea. Christiane stood there, motionless, staring at her friend.

"I'm not feeling too well, that's all. I'd better take a day or two off and get some rest," she managed to blurt out. But her face betrayed her. She wanted to hide her hurt, to escape, to avoid Christiane's inquisitive eyes. She wanted to be alone, to think things through.

Alice Gendron took the bus home. She lived in an apartment not far from the University of Ottawa. A handsome building, a bit old but clean and well kept. In the vestibule she came to a stop in front of the mailbox. Reluctant to open it, she hesitated for a moment, then dropped the key into her purse and headed for the stairs. Her apartment was just like her: clean and organized. Ever since she had become a nurse in Montreal she had worked and put money aside to buy a little home one day, a place where she could feel secure with Louise, somewhere she could relax after a long day's work.

The first years in Montreal had not been easy. She divided her time between work, housekeeping chores, and her daughter. She never saw Pierre again, and he never paid her a cent in child support. At first she attempted to seek him out, to talk to him, to smooth over their differences, but it had all been for naught. He wanted nothing to do with her.

As she slowly made her way up the stairs she remembered Pierre's eyes as he stared at her coldly, without emotion, as though they were total strangers, as though they had never lived and dreamed together.

"I've made up my mind. I'm going to keep the child," she'd

said in a quiet voice, head lowered, as they sat on a park bench watching children play in the sandbox.

Pierre had not answered. His lower jaw was trembling slightly. Then from between clenched teeth he said, "It's me or the baby. If you change your mind, you know where to find me." Then he got to his feet, turned on his heel, and walked away.

Alice watched the children at play and wiped the tears that trickled down her cheeks. A single thought flashed into her mind: *It will be the baby. Yes, it will be the baby.*

Alice laboriously lifted one foot and then the other. The stairs seemed steeper than usual, almost interminable. How far away all that seemed. She'd left Montreal, and in Ottawa she had found a wonderful job and a few good friends. And above all, her daughter, Louise, grew up peacefully, shining light every day on the dark pages of those black days.

Alice was panting. She took a deep breath and turned the key. As she opened the door, she felt as though she would collapse. No, it was not a bad dream—she was wide awake. There, standing in the middle of the living room, dressed in a strange costume, Louise was praying.

10

Emma felt lost in her new home. After three months at the women's shelter she'd lost the notion of personal space. During those hellish months she and Sara had felt crushed, suffocated, overwhelmed by the metal-framed beds and the dresser where they stored their belongings.

The new house was too big for her. And yet it was a small house, with a tiny kitchen, a ground-floor living room, and two bedrooms and a bathroom on the second floor. The stairway was narrow, the rooms cramped. The kitchen consisted of a counter held up by cabinets whose doors would barely close. Years of constant use had worn the floor bare.

And yet, Emma was happy. She hugged Sara tight, as if afraid of losing her in this still empty and soulless place. She'd double-locked the door. The neighbourhood didn't exactly inspire her with confidence. Tomorrow she would buy a security lock; that would put her at ease.

The living room was small but it had a large window that opened onto a minuscule backyard, the same kind of backyard she'd noticed when she came by for a look. Tucked up on one side and falling to the floor on the other, pink curtains bleached by the sun and covered with dust framed the window. The municipal employees who had cleaned the house before Emma's arrival surely thought it best to leave them as they were.

Emma walked towards the window, glancing furtively from side to side as if afraid of finding something untoward. Night was falling. At the rear of the yard she could make out a rusted bicycle and a bag of discarded junk. Weeds, dry and brittle, covered the ground, waiting to vanish with the first snow.

She stood still for a moment, lost in thought. Sara was sitting on the floor, leafing through some books she'd discovered in a cardboard box. All Emma could think about was her life over the past few years. Everything had happened so fast: graduation, the job of her dreams, her marriage to Fadi, Sara's arrival. She had been floating on a cloud of happiness; everything was beautiful, tinted in shades of pink. And then the wind had shifted. Things began to fall apart. Her descent into hell began.

One year after Sara's birth Emma was still torn. Should she stay at home with her daughter or return to work? Her job was demanding: she was an engineer working for a high-tech firm. Deadlines had to be met, and she feared she couldn't keep up the pace as well as look after her child. Her husband was indifferent. The idea of sending Sara off to daycare didn't seem to bother him; he insisted that Emma keep working.

But for Emma, the prospect of placing her daughter in some daycare centre while she continued to work exhausting hours was heartbreaking. Her sleep became troubled, and she began to resent her husband and his increasing obsession with his projects and his career. The Fadi of before seemed to be fading away. Day by day he was gradually turning into someone else. She knew it.

Was she to blame? Had Sara's birth turned their lives inside out? What had caused the rift that was now widening between them? Those were the questions that plagued Emma. Fadi, the easygoing young man she met during her last year at Montreal Polytechnic, was no longer the same.

She could see herself strolling beside him down Sainte-Catherine Street, watching the people rush by dressed in their office clothes, with serious expressions, their features strained by tension. Fadi was making humorous comments that made Emma burst out laughing, or telling stories of his childhood in Beirut.

"I remember clearly when the whole family would go out for a stroll after sunset along the Corniche. A mulberry-syrup seller had a stand there. I was wild about mulberry juice, so my father would buy me a glass. How I loved the sweet taste, and there was just a touch of sour that made me tingle..."

Emma listened attentively as she tried to imagine Fadi's favourite childhood haunts. Then he turned to her, looked her in the eyes, and said, "One day I'll take you to Lebanon. We'll stroll along the Corniche and watch the sun set behind the Pigeon Rocks at Raouché."

Emma blushed and said nothing, closing her eyes as if to capture the enchanting scene in her memory. As if to make good on his promise, he invited her then and there to a small Lebanese restaurant. He ordered two plates of shish taouk, rice, and green salad. When the dishes appeared, he made a face. "Like Mother always said, nothing can compare with the restaurants of Beirut, but you can always dream..."

They wolfed down the chunks of over-grilled chicken, the slightly glutinous rice, and the oily salad. They were so happy to be alone together that they hardly noticed the cheap meal in front of them. Emma, cheeks ablaze, was eating and giggling all at once.

But all that was dead now, dead and buried. As the years passed, the insouciant, optimistic young man with the ready smile had turned cold, calculating, unsmiling, attracted by the prospect of promotion and the lure of money. All that mattered was his ambition; his eyes were closed to the world around him. Only he counted.

Even though she could see him changing, Emma tried to pretend that nothing was wrong. She enrolled her daughter in a daycare and applied for transfer to a department where it would be easier for her to get home early and spend more time with Sara. She called her mother every weekend to tell her about her life, with all its ups and downs.

Fadi was increasingly withdrawing into a world of his own. Obsessed with his work, he paid no heed to his growing daughter, took nothing from those unforgettable years. Whenever Emma tried to talk to him about it, he got angry and flew into an odd rage, almost like madness. He justified himself by saying that he loved his daughter and no one was going to tell him how to feel. His arrogance grew. So disdainfully did he look down on everything and everyone that he never saw disaster lying in wait at his feet. Without realizing it, he had burned all his bridges: to his family, to his friends, and the last bridge, the one that connected him to his better self. He'd become vulnerable to the blows of life. He was at the mercy of the laws of the marketplace. Tragedy would not strike slowly.

When the high-tech bubble burst, there was no concealing the hard truth; layoffs quickly followed. They spared no one, from technicians to highly qualified engineers, from top management to clerical employees. Lean years followed hard on the heels of the high-living days when everyone in the high-tech sector dreamed of hitting the jackpot, of becoming a millionaire. Fadi had nurtured the illusion day and night—it became his objective, and he lived for it alone. Then, abruptly, Fadi the invincible, the high and mighty, saw his dreams crumble, disintegrate, and collapse in a cloud of dust. The fall was brutal, the noise deafening.

Emma tried to console him. She told him he would find another job and that they could get by on her salary. They had their daughter to think about. Maybe it had been a sign from God that they should rethink their priorities. But the rot had gone too deep. Fadi retreated into a stern and icy silence, broken only by outbursts of violent anger against Emma.

Their life became unbearable. Every day Emma felt more and more humiliated. There was no end to the psychological abuse. She could no longer work and no longer knew which way to turn. One day she picked up Sara from school and sought refuge at a women's shelter. There she filed for divorce.

11

Daddy dearest,

These days I'm writing my quarterly exams! Really tearing my hair out! But my courses are great. For sure I made the right choice when I registered for business administration. By the way, when will you be coming? Do try to find a way to drop off here, please; we haven't seen you since last summer. My childhood girlfriend Dina—you know, the tomboy—well, she went and got married! Unbelievable but true, I swear! We all attended the wedding. No big deal finally, everything went according to plan. In any event, nothing surprises me anymore, ever since Dina dropped everything to get married. Here the weather is starting to turn cold. It hasn't snowed yet, but any day now, I'm sure of it. I can't stand the heat in Dubai but I think I'm a bit jealous of you; these long, interminable winters of ours are starting to affect my system.

Looks like you're not quite as excited as before about the project we discussed over the phone. Are you still working at it or did you decide to let it drop? Lynne and Mona are fine.

*They say they're doing well at school and promised to write
you soon, but I'm not so sure. I'd better remind them of their
promise just in case . . .*

*Phew! These days we're not seeing as much of Leila as we
used to. Maybe Mommy has decided to keep her at a distance.
I hope so. I don't like her constant preaching. I think Mommy
is getting tired of those morning get-togethers of hers. Her heart
just isn't in it anymore.*

*How is your partner? Still the same old dim-witted ingrate?
I can't see why you don't move here, there are so many business
opportunities. I could give you a hand, and we'd be all together.*
Waiting impatiently for your answer,
Your dear daughter,
Lama

Lama wrote to her father with pen on paper. Even with
computers and email, she felt the need to communicate with
him that way. She could always find a quiet time, an empty
hour or even a few moments during a busy day, to write her
father a letter. A letter full of small talk and chit-chat in which
she kept him up-to-date on her life.

Her two sisters, Lynne and Mona, made fun of her: "You're
a throwback to the olden days. Why don't you use papyrus
or a quill pen?" But Lama paid no heed; she loved writing
to her father, even if everyone else found it faintly ridiculous. Besides, wasn't she the black sheep of the family, the
ugly duckling? To her mother and her sisters she was bizarre,
rebellious, a troublemaker, too old-fashioned in her ways, too
much of a hippie for their tastes, too open, but not up-to-date
enough to send her father a simple email.

Lama had long since made up her mind to ignore their carping. At first there were arguments, spats, and snide remarks, but she was determined to demonstrate how wrong her mother and sisters were. It was like an ongoing game, one in which she was determined to score enough points to win and prove how superior her point of view was. But over the past few weeks she'd changed her tactics. It wasn't premeditated; it all happened naturally, on its own. A curious silence had settled in and Lama no longer needed to win those tiny daily battles. She listened, but the impulse she'd had to answer back was no longer there. At last she stopped seeing her presence as a thorn in the family's side. Instead she sought peace at any price.

Lama was walking down the hall towards the main library. Her abundant, curly hair fell about her shoulders. She was about to pick up the pace when her eye caught a small poster taped to the wall: THE MUSLIM STUDENTS ASSOCIATION INVITES YOU TO JOIN AND TO PARTICIPATE IN IMPROVING LIFE FOR STUDENTS. COME VISIT US IN ROOM . . .

Lama jotted down the room number and continued on her way. She wasn't religious to the point of neglecting herself, but she was religious enough not to forget who she was, as she liked to put it. She was curious to find out about other Muslim students like herself, to share ideas, to participate in cultural events, even to put a little distance between herself and her mother and her friends.

For her, university was a golden opportunity to fly with her own wings, to find her way in the world, far from her mother's traditional views and far from the superficiality of her sisters and their entourage. She was determined to live life on her terms, not to let herself be trapped like Dina. She sped up; the library was not far off. The thought of Dina made her shiver. But no sooner had she sat down in front of a computer to begin work on her research project than she forgot all about Dina's story and plunged into her subject.

12

Fawzia Hussein was a simple woman, but there was nothing simple-minded about her. Ever since her daughter had thrown herself, body and soul, into religion, she had become sad and melancholy. Before, she would spend much of the day cooking spicy, savoury meals for her little family, and she would always send a nicely garnished portion to one of her neighbours. When she wasn't in the kitchen, she was in the sewing room, where she turned out tunics and trousers cut from the choicest fabrics in eye-pleasing colours. With the radio cassette player at her elbow playing an Indo-Pakistani melody, she would nod in time to the music. Her friends brought her fabrics whenever they returned from trips to their home villages. They would drop by to ask her to sew this or that dress or ensemble. Sewing was Fawzia's passion: she loved seeing a lifeless piece of fabric transformed in her hands into a nicely fitted tunic or a pretty pair of baggy trousers that were tight about the ankles.

But now Sally left her no room for happiness, for her small

daily pleasures. Her daughter's metamorphosis had cast a pall over everything she held dear; it had confiscated her right to dream and ripped open the fragile wrapping she'd enveloped herself in since her arrival in Canada. Fawzia could not resume her daily routine without thinking of Sally. At first she could not even look at her daughter clad in black from head to toe, walking down the street like a ghost. But it was Sally's attitude that disturbed her most of all. A kind of scorn, an expression of superiority on her face became more visible with every passing day. Her loving daughter, whom she had called the rose of her garden, had become a black spot, a discordant voice that sang out of tune in their household.

Fawzia was a pious woman who prayed and fasted. She was always ready to lend a hand to newly arrived immigrants. But was the Islam she practised any different from — or not as good as — the Islam Sally had recently discovered? She didn't read articles on the Internet the way her daughter did, of course. She had no idea what the *ulema* were saying on a whole variety of subjects. She continued to speak broken English with her neighbours, but everybody liked her, and no one had ever criticized her for being a bad Muslim — no one except Sally. Her daughter never missed a chance to point out that her headscarf had fallen to her shoulders or that her hair was showing or that she should raise her hands up to her ears to begin the prayer.

Sally made her comments with a coldness that tied her mother's stomach in knots. *Is this really the daughter I raised? Is this the same Sally who wrapped her little arms around me and twirled and spun in front of me to show off her dress?* she wondered, with brimming eyes. But last night, when she went to wish her daughter goodnight, Fawzia thought she'd caught a glimpse of the old sparkle. A wise, patient woman, she said nothing and asked no questions of her daughter. But before turning in, she prayed fervently, *Dear Lord, bring my Sally, my missing daughter, back to me...*

That night Sally could not sleep. She left her BlackBerry on the bedside table. It was all she could do not to reread the poem The Boy Next Door had sent her. Hadn't she promised that she wouldn't even think about it, would never reread those hellish words that had thrown her soul into an uproar and had transformed her into a non-believer? They weren't obscene words or even vulgar words, but when she heard them issuing from her mouth, she felt like a little girl caught stealing chocolate cookies by her mother. She felt so guilty that sleep was impossible.

Ever since discovering the straight path, Sally had spared no effort to study her religion and to learn the right way to pray. She divided her time between her courses and spiritual readings. She told herself she had no time to lose. This life was worthless — she must do everything to save her soul and those of her poor parents before Judgement Day. The articles she read gave her a strength she had never believed she possessed. No longer the spoiled little girl who got everything she wanted, she intended to prove to everyone how strong she was. Her decision to cover her face was only the first step. It would set her apart from the other girls, the ones who styled themselves Muslims but who were, in reality, sell-outs to the worlds of fashion and advertising.

Her way of dressing was her way of self-affirmation. Her fascination with technology was a divine blessing, a gift from

God that opened wide the doors of knowledge. Within the winding corridors of the Internet she'd been able to return to her roots, to rediscover true Islam. Not the Islam of the defeatists and the hypocrites, but an Islam that was unadulterated, rigorous. Not the Islam of political calculation and intrigue, but that of the Prophet Muhammad, peace be upon him, and his closest companions. Not the Islam of compromise that some *ulema* were trying to make people swallow, but a pure and intransigent Islam that would make not one single concession to softness. That poem had disturbed her best-laid plans.

Who was The Boy Next Door? What did he want? Should she ignore him or answer him? Would it be a sin to answer on her BlackBerry? She'd never seen a legal opinion on the subject. But wasn't the whole thing virtual in any event? The Boy Next Door couldn't see her, couldn't hear her voice. Would it do any harm? Would it be undermining one of the pillars of Islam if she were to answer him?

What if he was obsessed with sex, or a mental case? Sally shook her head. It couldn't be. Eloquent and intelligent words like those could not be the work of a low or evil mind. With a deliberate movement, she picked up her BlackBerry and removed it from its pink case, then scrolled through her inbox. She wanted to reread his words—perhaps she would discover a secret meaning. To her astonishment, up popped a new message from The Boy Next Door.

I call out to you, you flee.
Do not look far,
You're close to me.

Sally stopped in her tracks. It was impossible to go on. She felt queasy. She had to delete the message and forget the whole thing. But something held her back and she did nothing of the kind. She whispered a prayer, turned off the device, placed it back on her bedside table, and attempted to sleep.

13

Louise looked downright ridiculous in the new prayer outfit she'd bought at the Arab convenience store down the street, the one that sold halal meat and Middle Eastern spices but had recently begun to sell headscarves imported from Turkey and inexpensive prayer garments from the United Arab Emirates. It consisted of a long skirt, with an elasticized waistband, that came down to her ankles, and a large scarf with a hole in the middle that fitted over the face while the rest of the fabric covered her shoulders, arms, and midsection.

She was standing in the living room on the tiny silk carpet her mother had bought last year to bring herself "some pleasure after all the years of hard work," as she never tired of repeating. Louise knelt, forehead touching the floor, then got to her feet and bent over, her hands resting on her knees, then put her forehead to the floor once more, her mouth silently forming the words of the prayer. Her mother's sudden entry into the room released a bolt of tension. Pretending to be engrossed, Louise kept praying, but for all her efforts, her head began to spin.

Alice Gendron, lost in her memories and breathing heavily after climbing the stairs, began to seethe with anger at the sight of her daughter, dressed like a beggar, her eyes lowered in concentration, toes aligned on the handsome Persian carpet she'd worked so hard to buy. She wanted to explode in fury, to vomit up the words that seemed trapped in her throat, to free herself of the stress that had been building over the past weeks. She wanted to make a scene, to show Louise how much she was suffering deep down and how betrayed she felt. But she swallowed her hurt and rushed off to the refuge of her bedroom. It was strange — she simply didn't have the strength to force a confrontation.

Louise no longer knew what she was saying as she mechanically recited the words she'd memorized from the little book her friend Ameur had lent her. Her mother's unexpected appearance had had the effect of a volcanic eruption. Everything turned upside down in her mind; she didn't know whether to keep praying or to stop. The words to the prayers that she'd repeated so often and learned so well were swept away, as by a desert wind.

Louise was not afraid of her mother. She loved her, respected her, and was inspired by her, by the strength of her character and her willpower. She shared her hopes and fears, but she had never been afraid of her. Her mother was her best friend, the sister she'd never had, her missing father, everything. But ever since Louise had spoken openly of her wish to become a Muslim, things had changed. Alice no longer spoke to her as she once had. In fact, she was constantly angry at her, she of all people, who rarely judged anyone, even telling her, "Ever since you met that guy Ameur and his Muslim Students Association you've stopped thinking for yourself."

Her words hit Louise like poisoned darts piercing flesh. She would never have dreamed that her mother would speak to her that way, or that she would accuse her daughter of losing her discernment and her good judgement. This was the woman who had trained her almost from infancy to ask questions, to criticize, to take nothing for granted. This was the mother who had told her, time and time again, not to judge others before she knew them.

Louise had always applied those principles, and they had served her well. Her relations with her mother were calm, tender; the two were meant for each other, and no obstacle came between them, no cloud had ever darkened their clear blue sky. But since she had come to know Ameur and the other Muslim students, Louise and Alice were like strangers under the same roof. Louise spoke more and more of religion, and Alice felt increasingly ill at ease with every passing day.

It wasn't simply that Alice felt her past and all its unhappiness raising its ugly head. Rather it was the sinister, surreptitious invasion she sensed in the religion her daughter had accepted. Louise wanted to share with her mother what she had learned about Islam, but every day Alice withdrew further into her protective shell. She was certain that her daughter's curiosity would soon evaporate, that it was a flash in the pan. To her it was a passing identity crisis, a little like the young people of her own generation's fascination with communism: a passionate but ephemeral flirtation.

But for Louise it was a combination of love and faith. The attraction she felt for Ameur and for his words, and the way he lowered his gaze timidly when he spoke to her—it was a search for her missing father, for her missing faith, for a passion for the divine, for all that she had never experienced, never felt. Her mother had always given her the right to choose, but this time it was different. Now she wanted to pluck the fruit that had been forbidden to her. Louise found herself up against a wall that she was not even allowed to touch.

Alice had waited patiently for things to calm down, for her daughter to return naturally to the right path. But instead, things took a turn for the worse. The pot was about to overflow. Louise had become a Muslim, a practising believer—exactly what Alice loathed most in this world.

When she'd finished her prayer, Louise touched her forehead to her mother's beautiful Persian carpet and whispered, "Help me, dear God. Give me strength and courage and soften my mother's heart." Then she stood up, removed her prayer garment, folded it up, and went to place it in her wardrobe.

Her mother had seen her praying. The two women kept a wary eye on one another like two hens, each in her corner of the room, ready to attack. But neither dared to confront the other. Louise did not know if her mother would continue to tolerate her presence. Alice looked on as her daughter sunk deeper and deeper, day by day, into that foreign religion of hers. Without saying a word, the two expected the worst. Louise's love for her mother tormented her, and so did her new life as a Muslim. Alice was torn between maternal love and her personal convictions. The two suffered in silence. And they waited, watchful.

Louise was deeply attached to both Ameur and her mother. She did not want to lose either. She wished only that her mother could accept what she had become. Ameur gave her his full support but said she had to be patient with her mother—even though she was a non-believer, she must not be harsh with her. That advice transformed Ameur into a hero in Louise's eyes, a noble and gallant Prince Charming who extended his hand even to those who despised him.

"Only a few months more, then I'll finish my degree and by the grace of God we'll marry, I promise." Louise lived with those sweet words in her mind, and with the hope that her mother would change her mind and accept her choice.

14

"You call those marks? Don't stare at me like innocent victims! Aren't you ashamed of yourselves?"

Mrs. Bibi was beside herself. Her half-smoked cigarette lay smouldering in the a crystal ashtray that refracted the rays of the afternoon sunlight against onto the white walls of the living room. Lynne and Mona, her two youngest daughters, stared at her in stunned silence. Both had just come home with catastrophic marks in math—they hadn't even understood the questions.

Mrs. Bibi had long since forgotten that when she was a girl, she hated math, in addition to not understanding it. "Just imagine what your father will say! I can hear it all now: 'Here I am, killing myself on the job so I can send you money, and what do you do? You spend all your time partying and neglecting your studies.' What am I supposed to tell him, eh? You tell me. And you can wipe that expression off your faces. You make me want to slap you!"

Lynne, the elder of the two, broke into sobs, counting on

their mother to pity them. It was her way of dodging shouting and punishment, and it never failed. Mona, indifferent, stared at the floor, waiting for the storm to blow over; it was all a question of time, and she knew it. Their mother would call one of her friends and finally calm down. They had only to wait out the roar of thunder and the flashes of lightning and keep their mouths closed.

But Mrs. Bibi was not about to stop. She'd had her fill of her daughters, her fill of raising three daughters on her own in Canada, her fill of a husband who left her with all the responsibility while he continued to work abroad and didn't make the slightest effort to get a job here. And she'd had her fill of Lama, who instead of helping her out like a mature, responsible girl, was still wearing torn jeans and reading books by "diabolical" authors. In fact, she'd had her fill of everybody and everything.

She seemed to forget that she was the one who had insisted on buying their luxurious house. Or that she was the one who organized morning get-togethers to dazzle her friends and parade her newest acquisitions, and she couldn't stop buying new dresses and new furniture she didn't need for the sole purpose of being like the other women, or feeling superior to them.

Actually, Samia couldn't have cared less about her daughters' marks. She was so busy during the day, between the kitchen and the shopping, that when evening rolled around, she would flopped down in front of the television set for a bit of relief.

The programs on the Arab satellite channels were her favourites. You could find everything: song-and-dance shows featuring the Lebanese version of *Star Academy*, where inter-changeable nymphets with their brilliant artificial smiles paraded in front of the camera, dreaming of stardom. She adored old Egyptian films that made her weep and reminded her of her youth in Kuwait. But what she liked best of all were the programs of religious instruction, given by a scholar with a long beard and a grim look on his face who made threaten-ing gestures and had a laptop in front of him to answer view-ers' questions. She would break out in goosebumps and tears streamed down her cheeks. On the spot she would vow to never again miss a prayer. But the next day, after a late night, as she struggled to get up for the pre-dawn prayer, she would forget the sheikh's message, curse her life, and plunge back into sleep as if nothing the sheikh said had left a trace in her heart.

In her fury, Mrs. Bibi seemed to forget the hidden side of her life. It was enough to shout her rage at her two younger daughters. Lynne and Mona would hang their heads dutifully, and then, to reward them for their obedience and devotion, she would buy them whatever they desired.

But with Lama the situation was far more complex. She was out of reach. "You're the spitting image of your father, the way you run away from people, your antisocial ways...Ah, I pity the man who marries you!" Mrs. Bibi would hammer away at her, never missing an opportunity.

The truth was that her daughters' poor marks hardly bothered her, no more than her husband's reaction, for that matter. Long ago she had learned how to tame him, how to smooth over situations without getting involved in intermin-able squabbles. His distance, his remoteness, which she complained so bitterly about, actually worked to her advantage. Her husband was completely caught up in business, and he had better be. His role was to work and send money to his family so that they would want for nothing.

Mrs. Bibi was furious because her daughters' bad marks had disturbed her carefully constructed facade of normality, a virtual world that provided her with a bit of happiness and stability. The incident had brought her back to reality, and that was what irritated her. It was a mournful and fetid reality that Mrs. Bibi could not accept, that she loathed, just as she had loathed her childhood behind the white walls of the huge family home, with its windows covered by drawn curtains. Her absent parents, her thirst to be loved, to be embraced, and most of all, the rootless feeling that she felt, the little Palestinian who had never seen the land of her ancestors, were like a crushing burden on her frail shoulders. Then there was the rejection by her Kuwaiti playmates, who looked down on her as if she were a stateless beggar who had come to profit from their wealth and to steal their resources.

All of those things Mrs. Bibi kept hidden deep inside her, burying her memories in a deep shaft where the light never shined. She surrounded herself with false friends. Flooded Lynne and Mona with superfluous purchases to distract them from their problems. Smothered Lama's every attempt at rebellion, the better to conceal her own defeat.

The bad grades had inflicted nasty scratches on the smooth surface of her life. She had to find a proper solution, fast.

She called Leila and asked for advice, which her friend was quick to provide. "But what kind of world are you living in, sweetie? All children need private coaching these days. How did your daughters get this far without it? Math is hard, not to mention that it's in English. You should hire a private tutor as soon as possible. All is not lost, the school year is just beginning. You're fortunate..."

Mrs. Bibi was hesitant. "A man to tutor my daughters? And what if something happened? No, I could never accept that."

Leila was not about to give up. Mrs. Bibi could not imagine where she'd dug up so many arguments. But she wasn't about to let the girls' math marks take over her life, so gradually she let herself be convinced. When she put down the handset on the mahogany coffee table, her mind was made up.

She would take out a classified ad in the local newspaper. Surely her husband wouldn't say a word if she explained that she needed money to pay for private lessons for their daughters. And she would find a female tutor, to avoid problems. She felt better already; her cheeks were shining once more. She pulled a package of cigarettes from the imitation Louis Vuitton bag she'd bought in Kuwait, took one out, lit it with her gold-plated lighter, and inhaled slowly, deeply. The storm was already receding.

15

Emma walked her daughter to the school-bus stop. Now that she'd left her husband she no longer had a car. That was behind her now. She wanted nothing to do with Fadi; all she wanted was peace of mind.

A handful of parents were waiting at the bus stop already. There wasn't a white face among them; they were all Asians or blacks. The Asians, originally from China or Vietnam, lived in the fine big houses that Emma could see from her tiny backyard. The blacks, from Somalia, lived in the same social housing as Emma.

The two contingents of children pulled and tugged at one another, laughing, as they waited for the bus. Their parents chatted with other people of their ethnic group. Emma, hair covered with a headscarf and with pale skin that set her apart, kept her distance. She held Sara's hand, looking impatiently down the street for the yellow bus that would take her daughter to school. Sara, tiny and frail in her winter coat, watched the other children squabbling with an amused look on her

face. It was clear that she wanted to take part in their innocent little disturbance, but her shyness held her back. It was
enough to watch and listen to the children's gestures and
excited chatter.

The bus pulled up and the door swung open. The group
calmed down, and the children moved close to mothers
or fathers as though they had suddenly remembered they
would be separated for the day. Emma kissed her daughter, checked to make sure all her buttons were fastened, and
waited patiently while Sara found a seat on the bus. She sat
down next to a window and flattened her nose against the
glass, smiling at her mother with her tiny white teeth. Emma
waved at her and felt tears welling in her eyes. A pang of fear
at being alone pierced her stomach, but she let nothing show,
and continued to wave goodbye to Sara until the school bus
drove off, leaving a cloud of grey exhaust fumes in its wake.

Emma returned to her new home. It no longer felt empty,
as it had for the first few days after the move. She'd bought
some used furniture: a kitchen table, a sofa, and bookshelves.
She had also purchased plates, drinking glasses, and a few
pots and pans for the kitchen. There was a room for her, and
one for her daughter, and each of the bedrooms was furnished
with a mattress and a chest of drawers. It was simple, modest,
and clean.

For all her sadness, Emma grew more attached to the place
with every passing day. For her it represented a break with her
husband's psychological abuse, with his indifference and his
obsessive, pathological ambition. The scene was always the
same, and Fadi's words echoed still in her ears.

"There you go, imagining things, looking for problems

everywhere. Sara is just fine. You're the one who's not fine."

Emma answered back, her voice quavering with emotion. "But Sara is *our* daughter. You can't leave her to grow up all alone. You have to help...we have to make sacrifices together."

He looked at her darkly. "You seem to forget that I must complete my project at all costs. I've got to get my promotion. You have no right to keep me from advancing in my career with all these preposterous and imaginary pretexts—"

Emma couldn't hold back. "I have every right to remind you of your duties as father and husband. Why should I be the only one to look after Sara? She needs you too, doesn't she?"

Fadi was losing patience. His eyes burned with anger, and in a loud voice he said, "You're afraid of everything. You can't manage your stress, you panic over nothing, you're depressed. Go see a shrink—" He stopped in mid-sentence. Lifting his hand in exasperation, he leaped to his feet and stormed out, slamming the door behind him.

Emma wanted to plug her ears. For months Fadi had been insulting her and hurting her feelings. He ridiculed her, called her stupid, crazy, and paranoid. And whenever she wanted to talk with him, to tell him that it was high time he began to look after Sara and her, he wriggled away, turned his back and ran, seeking refuge in the virtual world of his job that would soon betray him.

The separation had been abrupt and painful. Emma had seen it coming but had done everything in her power not to look. She had tried to convince herself that Fadi would change, that he would come to his senses, but things only got worse. There was no going back.

Today she was a divorced woman with a child, educated but without a job, an immigrant without family. During their weekly phone conversations, her mother begged her to return to her homeland to live. "You don't have a husband; you're a single mother with a young child. You don't even have a job. Why do you keep insisting you want to live there?"

The same question, over and over again. Emma pondered her mother's words and weighed them carefully. She had gone over them what seemed like hundreds of times, but never did she make up her mind to leave Ottawa and return to Tunis. Was it fear of being singled out as the model girl who'd failed? Was it apprehension about returning to live in the country she'd left years ago, one that represented a distant past? All she knew was that she was going to stay where she was. She had no intention of giving in to her mother's demands. For her, only one thing mattered: Sara's well-being.

Emma sat down on the striped sofa, which smelled of age and household cleaner. She picked up the neighbourhood weekly, on the lookout for a job that would bring her a little more money to meet her needs. She'd lost her former job as a programmer, but in her current circumstances she couldn't begin looking for a full-time position. What she needed was work that would restore her self-confidence and bring in enough money to supplement her monthly welfare cheque.

She scanned the classified ads. They wanted truck drivers, people to hand out advertising flyers, painters, but for there was nothing for someone with her academic qualifications. She heard a little laugh from deep inside: *So that's why you came to study in Canada, eh? What happened to that computer engineering degree of yours, to all those years you worked like a madwoman?*

Is that why you made all the sacrifices . . . to end up on welfare, read-ing the classified ads hoping to find some crummy job where you'll be treated like a servant? What are you doing here, anyway? Why don't you go home to your mother? You could find a job in a flash back there, enrol your daughter in a private school, forget Fadi and maybe even find a husband, an easygoing Tunisian who wouldn't hold your past against you, who'd help you heal your old wounds . . .

Emma closed her eyes. She recognized that high-pitched, nasal voice. It made her suffer, tormented her, kept her awake at night. She shook her head, as though that alone would turn off the mocking voice, and resumed scanning the classifieds. It was then that she spotted the ad: FAMILY SEEKS INSTRUCTOR TO GIVE PRIVATE LESSONS IN MATHEMATICS TO TWO HIGH-SCHOOL STUDENTS, GRADE 10 AND 11. CALL EVENINGS AT . . .

She jotted down the number in her datebook. *Why not?* she mused. *I've taken so many math courses I could teach at any level.* Then she remembered Sara. *Where would I leave her? No, no way I could leave her here alone. Yes, she'll have to come with me . . . that will be my only condition . . .*

Reassured by her own words, she put down the paper and went into the kitchen to prepare a spaghetti sauce for tonight's meal. Sara loved pasta. She punched the On but-ton of her cassette player, and the nostalgic, cajoling music broke the silence of the house. Emma hummed the refrain. The spiteful little voice inside her had quieted, overcome by a murmur of happiness . . .

16

The fervent messages continued to accumulate in Sally's inbox. She was less and less sure of what she should do. First she had been afraid to read them for fear of committing a sin, and now she read them again and again until she knew them by heart. They were poems, attractive, well written. Their author was begging her to reply.

Sally hesitated as if paralyzed. Those messages touched her as nothing had before. They enveloped her in a cloak of love or, better, chipped away at the hard shell of coldness and rigidity that she'd built up around her. Their words resonated deep within her, leaving her at wit's end. She struggled against her emotions, attempted to bury them deep in a rocky, arid garden plot where, against all expectations, they burst into strong and vigorous flower.

Now Sally — who had nothing but criticism for her parents, who accused them of being too soft, too permissive, of flirting dangerously with disbelief and disobedience to God — had no idea what she should do. These messages from an unknown person had turned everything inside her upside down. Was it curiosity? Was it the beginnings of love that had undermined her devotion, or had her soul been overcome by temptation? Sally knew only one thing: whenever she received a message from her unknown admirer, her heart began to throb violently, her hands grew moist, and she felt as though she was ascending to heaven!

Every day Sally waited impatiently for a message, counting the minutes and the hours until it popped up on her BlackBerry. She reflected long and hard on every word she read, savouring them like the tastiest ice cream. Then she made ready to type out an answer, only to hesitate at the last minute. The words of her sheikh's sermon rang in her ears and the verses of the Qur'an filed through her mind.

Just the day before, she had participated in an online discussion on the advisability of both men and women attending a marriage ceremony. Sheikh Abdurrahman Bilal was categorical: *It is forbidden to attend marriage ceremonies where men and women are seated together. Whatever the ceremony, any occasion where men and women meet to eat, dance, listen to music is forbidden. It is an illicit environment that our young men and women must be spared.*

One of the participants, called Jinane, who Technogirl always found had pertinent comments to make on virtual forums, asked a question: *What if the women are seated on one side of the room, and men on the other? Is it permitted to attend such a ceremony?*

The sheikh was even more intransigent. *The answer is no! Women must be in a separate room*, he quickly fired back.

What about music at a party for women only? asked Didi,

another regular participant, who liked to ask ambiguous questions on various forums. Technogirl, for reasons unknown to her, particularly disliked her.

At that the sheikh wheeled out his heavy artillery, running through narratives attributed to the Prophet, warning all participants in the forum against music and the wiles of Satan. As she read the words, Sally gulped painfully. She had no idea what she should do. It was as if the question hardly concerned her. After all, she did not listen to music and read only the poetic words of The Boy Next Door.

Each time she glanced at one of his messages, Sally was transfixed for hours. The only way to put them out of her mind was to get back to her books. And to think that she'd once considered giving up her worldly education to devote herself full-time to studying religion!

When Sally announced that she planned to give up her courses in computer programming at the University of Ottawa, her parents were not intimidated. They had no intention of leaving the choice to her, as they had with the niqab. More, they brought up several arguments to prove their point: not only was she committing no sin, the search for knowledge was a religious duty. It wasn't the same kind of opposition that had followed her decision to wear the niqab. Then, their objections had been timid and confused. No, this time they were adamant. Their opposition was fierce and unbending in defence of what little remained of their dream, like a still-leafy branch hanging from a tree just charred by lightning. They grasped it with all their might. Sally's academic career represented the years of sacrifice since they'd immigrated to Canada. They had invested their sweat, their savings, their reputation, and the best of themselves. Then had come her caprices, the life choices that left them stunned and heartbroken. They were determined not to allow Sally to run roughshod over them.

This time Sally didn't have a chance. Her parents wouldn't make any concessions. Cornered, heavy-hearted, she signed up for her final session at the university. But with her gifts and enthusiasm for computers, she quickly got down to work and forgot that just a few months before she had almost—on her own initiative—put an end to the long years of study and toil.

She had been sitting in front of her computer since early morning, working on her session project. As she reflected on how proud she was of her work, a thought flashed across her mind. She had no idea by what mental process she remembered a phrase that The Boy Next Door, her secret admirer, used frequently: *In my thoughts, you are / like a precious stone...* Turning away from the keyboard, she stood up and walked over to the mirror.

Her room contained a large bed and the worktable where she kept her computer. She had removed all the pictures that had been hanging on the wall since her childhood. They were *haram*, a form of adoration of things created by man that turned people away from their ultimate purpose—the adoration of God, the One and Only. Even the collection of miniature elephants carved from wood that her mother had given her for her sixteenth birthday lay hidden deep in one of the drawers of her night table. Sally had adored those little elephants, especially the extraordinary attention to detail. The sight of them, all different sizes, one behind another, tails hanging down and tusks raised high, reminded her of her parents' native Asia. In them she saw her roots, a sense of discipline side by side with untamed nature.

But ever since Sally had discovered the true faith, she never once restored those impious statuettes to her night table. When she consulted her favourite website, she learned that keeping them was a form of *shirk*, pure polytheism. *Idol worship*, her favourite sheikh had declared without a moment's hesitation. She wanted to throw them into the wastebasket straightaway but she just couldn't bring herself to do it. Instead she placed them in a box, which she consigned to the bottom of the drawer. There, in the darkness, far from her eyes, those symbols could have no effect on her faith. She did not want to look at her carved wooden elephants again; they only reminded her of her futile attachment to material things.

In one corner of the room stood a bookcase where religious books rubbed shoulders with computer manuals. Sally's two great loves: faith and computing. Standing in front of the mirror, Sally scrutinized herself. Her jet-black hair framed a diminutive, fine-featured face. Her black eyes stood out against her pale skin. But those same soft eyes gave off an artificial severity. It was a severity that gave her the appearance of a confused young girl searching for identity, crying out for moral support.

Sally stared long and hard at her reflection in the mirror, so long that she forgot about her project, which was due soon. Picking up a stick of black kohl, she swept it across her eyelids. Deftly she repeated the movement, as if to ensure that the black pencil had left its mark. Focusing once more on the face in the mirror, she was surprised at how much more mature she looked, how different from the clumsy adolescent of only a few minutes before. The words of The Boy Next Door echoed in her mind:

Beneath your black veil
I see your body
Patiently I wait in my corner
Perhaps one day I will be yours

At that moment her BlackBerry began to vibrate. Her stomach knotted and she sighed. Then she turned towards it in haste, anxious to see who had sent her a message.

17

Louise had met Ameur at the University of Ottawa, where they had enrolled in the same biology course. She wanted to become a nurse like her mother. Ameur had signed up to complete the course requirements for his undergraduate biology degree and planned to enrol in med school.

Ameur's parents were Egyptians who had been living in Canada for quite a few years. Ameur had been born in Ottawa and had always lived there. He was a dynamic young man, very active in the university Muslim student organization, and an excellent speaker. Words flowed from his mouth like the clear, fast-flowing waters of a mountain stream. He had a talent no one could deny. His curly hair was closely cut and his sparse beard was barely visible; with his dark skin he could have been Mexican. Ameur was a good practising Muslim: he didn't go out with girls, didn't drink, and spent most of his time studying or managing the Muslim Students Association, of which he was president.

His only secret was that he wanted to marry a girl with blue eyes. It was a lifelong dream that he'd never spoken to anyone about, not even his mother, Fatma, who had raised him to respect their traditions and their religion. Ameur knew that he wouldn't be committing a sin, that his thoughts were pure, and that one day, God willing, his wish would come true in full legitimacy and with the benediction of his parents. All he had to do was find a young Muslim wife with blue eyes. When he met Louise, it was love at first sight. All he could see was her eyes. He dared not look her over—that would be against the precepts of his religion—but his furtive glances inspired him to dream of Louise and of the day when they would be married.

One day Ameur and Louise found themselves in the same group for a class project. Alice Gendron, Louise's mother, would call it pure coincidence, but Ameur was certain that God had brought him and Louise together. She was attracted by the way he spoke: no sooner did he open his mouth than she stopped whatever she was doing to listen to him. He switched readily from French to English, and he could explain concepts to Louise that would have taken her days to comprehend. That was Ameur's way of courting her. Nothing dangerous, nothing illicit. Just words.

But gradually the words evolved into conversations, and then into meetings. Ameur didn't want to give Satan an opportunity to tempt him, so he arranged to see Louise in the university cafeteria, at the library, or in the Muslim Students Association office. The two of them were never alone together. They chatted about their courses, but Louise wanted to know more about Ameur, about his principles, his values. He was different from the others. It wasn't his physical presence or his exotic appearance that drew her to him, but the way he'd been raised, what he believed in, his goals in life.

Ameur never missed an opportunity to tell her about Islam, about the pillars of the faith, about the moral standards it propounded and the prejudices that surrounded it. He gave her books that she devoured in a day or two and that made her ask even more questions. Ameur wanted what was best for Louise. He dreamed of the day when he could marry her, the girl with the blue eyes.

Louise had discovered Ameur and Islam at the same time. With every passing day she became more attached to both. At first she was drawn more strongly to Ameur, to his manners, his way of speaking, his intelligence, but gradually she discovered Islam and could no longer do without it. She read whatever came her way, whatever helped her deepen her knowledge. She had a thirst that could not be quenched. Her mother had brought her up far from religion because she wanted her daughter to be free. Of course Louise felt free, but she also felt a yawning void deep inside her. She hadn't found a satisfactory answer to the questions of death and human suffering. With the Muslim religion she felt more enlightened and ready to face the existential questions that were tormenting her. She had found the spiritual reassurance that she had been seeking.

Ameur did his best to calm Louise's new-found religious enthusiasm. He reminded her how important it was to respect, to obey, and to please her mother. Patience would help her avoid many errors. "Be patient, and God will reward you," he told her. But Ameur's gallant and delicate manner swept her away. She could feel the flame of her faith swaying at his words; calmed, she let herself be soothed by the magic of his speech. She listened religiously, like a little girl, as he talked, and resolved to wait until her relationship with her mother improved.

It got worse instead. A year after meeting Ameur, Louise decided to become a Muslim. She had reached the point of no return. She was full of self-assurance — her new faith gave her life meaning. Ameur supported her in her first moments of doubt, but he had also spoken to her about the challenges her decision would force her to confront. Time and again he insisted that she must convert not for his sake but out of conviction.

Louise was happy to have encountered faith and love at the same time. She knew that Ameur's love was enough for her, that she did not have to venture onto the shifting and controversial ground of faith. Why had she crossed the line that separates emotion from spirituality? *Isn't it a sign from God who, in His wisdom and knowledge, made Ameur the instrument that guided me to the Truth?* she reassured herself, as if to banish all doubt.

Unfortunately, her mother saw things quite differently. She hated that her daughter had fallen for that boy. She was convinced he had cast a spell over Louise. She believed fervently in the principles of secularism, of equality between the sexes, and of the primacy of law over religion. It was clear that her daughter's conversion was a sign of submission and servitude, a shameful surrender of her freedom. This woman, who had stood tall and made her own way, saw in Louise's behaviour a flagrant example of dependency. A grave mistake. A death sentence . . .

18

Emma was on the bus. Sara was seated next to her, looking at the pictures in a children's book. The big day had come. She was on her way to Samia Bibi's house to meet her daughters, Lynne and Mona, and hopefully to begin tutoring them in math. She, the queen of bad luck, couldn't have expected better. For an engineer who ate numbers for breakfast, what could be easier than coaching two teenagers?

Mrs. Bibi had seemed pleasant enough on the phone, and very accommodating. "Of course there's no problem. You can bring your daughter along. Both of you are welcome."

What more could Emma want? An Arab Muslim family would pay her bus fare and for the time she would spend helping their two daughters with math in order to bring up their test scores. She couldn't have been happier. She was about to break out of the isolation she'd fallen into after her divorce and her move to the new neighbourhood.

For the occasion she had put on one of the suits she used to wear to work. She even applied a bit of makeup to hide the pallor of her cheeks—she wanted to look her best. Mrs. Bibi's house was at the other end of town, an hour's bus ride. *It's nothing. I'll have something to look at, and Sara will amuse herself during the ride,* thought Emma.

Sara was delighted to be accompanying Emma, but most of all she was happy that her mother was returning to life, reborn after so many months of pain and solitude. Sara was young, but sensitive. Instinctively she understood much of what her mother was going through. The breakup of the family and the months they'd spent in the shelter had brought them closer together; they'd become partners. As Sara leafed through her book, her eyes gleamed and a faint smile played across her tiny lips.

The streets of Ottawa had begun to fill with cars, taking people home after another day's work. Emma knew this part of town only vaguely. Staring off into the distance, she watched the houses and the vehicles speeding by. Finally the bus came to a stop at the corner she was looking for. Emma took her daughter's hand and they got off. A chilly wind was blowing and stray snowflakes clung to their clothing or fluttered to the sidewalk. Sara stuck out her tongue to catch one. Emma hurried; she wanted to arrive on time.

Mrs. Bibi's residence was located on a dead-end street, an island of quiet and luxury. It was a large house with a white stone facade. Sculpted lions guarded the massive wooden front door, a reminder of the house's original Italian owners. Stray dry leaves whirled across the grass, and bushes wrapped in heavy grey fabric reminded her of huge eggs. Emma rang the doorbell. The few seconds she waited seemed like an eternity; her knees felt weak.

Then the door opened and a slender, made-up woman emerged from behind it: Mrs. Bibi. "Welcome, Emma, come on in." Then she looked down at Sara. "This is your daughter? Oh, what a cutie! Mona, Lynne, come! Mrs. Emma is here."

With one hand Mrs. Bibi patted Sara's head and with the other closed the front door, her voice carrying as far as the top of the stairs. Lynne and Mona, who were standing there, exchanged glances, grimaced, and then made their way downstairs to join their mother and their new tutor.

The luxury dazzled Emma. It was as though she had stepped into a palace straight out of *The Thousand and One Nights*. Never had she seen such an immense house. Everything about it breathed wealth, from the furniture to the white marble floor, the carpets, and the soaring ceilings. The decor was an extravagant combination of styles, colours, and fabrics. Emma felt intimidated and confused. She followed Mrs. Bibi without uttering a word. She was not certain she wanted to work for these people. But the little voice deep inside her was quick to pipe up: *It's your chance to earn a little money, to pull yourself out of the solitude that's dragging you down day by day. Don't miss your chance!*

Mrs. Bibi was almost beside herself, delighted to have found a female teacher who was an Arab and a Muslim to help her two daughters master mathematics. She wouldn't have to worry her head because they would have better marks soon. She led Emma and Sara into a smaller room. There the furniture was simple compared to the luxury of the entry hall.

Mrs. Bibi motioned to Emma to sit down and they faced one another. "Would you like something to drink? Some mango juice, a cup of tea, some Turkish coffee perhaps?"

Emma did not know what to say and Sara remained silent. Not waiting for their response, Mrs. Bibi excused herself and left the room. Lynne and Mona made their appearance. They greeted Emma politely and sat down on the sofa across the room from her.

Emma attempted to dissipate the artificial shyness of the two teenagers. "So, you're in grades ten and eleven?" she asked them, as if to confirm what she already knew.

"I'm in grade eleven," said Lynne nonchalantly.

"And I'm in ten," Mona continued coolly.

They were both wearing tight jeans and bright-coloured sweaters that made them look alike, although Lynne was round-faced while Mona's features were a bit more angular. Emma asked them about their math courses and what they found difficult. The girls gave detailed answers but showed no enthusiasm.

Mrs. Bibi reappeared, carrying a large silver tray with a teapot, two porcelain cups, a bottle of water and a bottle of juice, and a plate of cookies. She filled a glass with juice and handed it to Sara, who didn't budge, glancing self-consciously at her mother for permission. Emma smiled at her and Sara picked up the glass, muttering a barely audible thank-you. Mrs. Bibi poured two cups of tea, one for herself and one for Emma, which she placed on the small table beside her.

Out of the corners of their eyes Lynne and Mona were looking Emma over from head to toe, as if they hardly knew what to think. Judging by her questions she seemed smart enough, but she looked dated to them, a bit schoolmarmish in her grey suit and badly fastened headscarf, as if she'd just stepped out of a old-fashioned book. Their mother ignored them, offering them neither tea nor cookies. It was Emma who interested her.

"Have you had a chance to talk with the girls? What do you think? Would you like to start next week?"

Her questions came thick and fast, hardly leaving Emma the time to think.

Lynne chewed on her right thumbnail while Mona scrutinized the ceiling. Sara sipped at her glass of mango juice. Head lowered, she examined the flower pattern of the carpet at her feet.

Emma hesitated for a moment, then said, "I'm an engineer by training. I can certainly tutor your daughters in math. I can come every Saturday afternoon, one hour for Lynne and one hour for Mona. And if they need help, they can always call me."

A cloud of disappointment passed over Mona's face, but she continued to study the ceiling. Lynne stopped biting her thumbnail. A radiant smile illuminated Mrs. Bibi's features. The two girls stood up and left the room without a goodbye.

Mrs. Bibi asked Emma, "Would two hundred dollars a week suit you?"

Sara was still staring at the carpet. She thought she could make out a large bird with round eyes, a long beak, and wide-spreading wings.

Delighted, Emma accepted; it was a godsend in these difficult times. She motioned to Sara that it was time to leave. Her daughter forgot her imaginary designs and got up.

A surge of warmth spread throughout Emma's body. Was it from the overheated room or from embarrassment? She couldn't tell. She thanked Mrs. Bibi and turned towards the entry hall, Sara following silently along behind her. Mrs. Bibi handed her a cookie. Sara smiled and put it in her pocket.

Outside, a fine coating of snow covered the walk. From the first-floor window Mrs. Bibi watched the two silhouettes as they moved away, side by side. Rapidly their footsteps in the newly fallen snow vanished in the gathering darkness.

19

Sally believed she'd solved the puzzle of the anonymous virtual love letters. At least she thought she had. Who else could it be but that skinny, solitary boy who sat in the last row of her computer science course, the one who was always gazing off into space? It had to be him. Sally couldn't prove it; it was just a hunch, of course. But she couldn't rid herself of the thought, and with every passing day it became more and more of a reality. Whenever she received an anonymous message, it was as though she could hear him reading it. She would imagine his shy mouth, his pallid face, and the long, fine hair that almost hid his eyes.

There were moments when she had her doubts. Why should she have such vain thoughts? Why would a non-Muslim boy be interested in her, a Muslim wearing a niqab? She knew the boy's name; it was Sam. She remembered the day when she'd stayed on after the lecture to copy down some notes from the blackboard. Sam had walked by in front of her and she'd had a feeling he wanted to talk to her. But she kept her head lowered and he continued on his way towards the exit.

But how did he get her email address? Why wasn't he interested in a normal girl — a white girl who didn't hide her entire body, who didn't have a mother who wore traditional Pakistani dress and a father who drove a taxi? Sally had no answer. She was deeply troubled. How could she be certain that those messages were coming from Sam?

Ever since the messages had broken through into her universe, Sally had felt as though she was becoming less strict in the practice of her religion. She did her prayers on time, read the Qur'an, listened to the sermons of her favourite sheikh, and proudly wore her niqab to university and didn't let a single hair show, as was her custom. She participated in her forums on the Web and condemned the laxity of so many Muslims, the way they rejected the fundamental values of Islam. As recently as yesterday she had written, as Technogirl, *Only a return to the fundamental values of Islam, to the traditions of our Prophet, peace be upon him, and of his first companions and the Holy Book can guide us in this world of perversity...*

But deep inside, Sally knew that she had strayed from her path. Her heart was not as pure as it had been before those messages of love. Their lovely words had touched her deeply, as though she had let fine and gentle strange hands caress her body. She was flirting with the forbidden while not straying too far. Time and again she had sworn not to read the messages, but it was no use. The anonymous words drew her to them. She could no longer get them out of her mind. Her fervent promises of the night would evaporate the next morning when the first lines of verse appeared on the screen of her BlackBerry.

Fawzia Hussein was aware of her daughter's transformation. Sally had become more amenable, less severe towards her and her husband. She no longer seized every opportunity to sermonize. She even ceased reminding her parents that the mortgage they'd signed years ago to purchase their house was *haram*. She stopped talking about Heaven and Hell. She stopped pointing out to her mother that her headscarf had slipped down and was showing her henna-tinted grey hair. Other things were clearly on Sally's mind. She smiled more often, became angry less often. Almost like the daughter she had once been — except, of course, for the long black robe she wore, and the headscarf that covered her entire face except for the eyes.

Fawzia could not have known what lay behind Sally's transformation. For her there could be only one reason: God had answered her prayers. Gradually she rediscovered the little pleasures that had deserted her when Sally took the niqab. Once again she resumed her little routines as she prepared Sally's favourite dishes. From the kitchen came the sound of Pakistani music, the old songs she loved, and the pungent odour of spices pervaded the house. She hustled back and forth between the oven, the fridge, and the pantry. Once more she was the queen of her realm. The unhappiness of the past was all but forgotten.

20

Alice Gendron's mind was made up: she was determined to lance the boil, to drain the pus, and find relief. It was high time she stopped denying how serious things had gotten. She had to talk to Louise the way she used to, before Louise met that guy Ameur and, along with him, that new religion of hers.

Alice was itching for a faceoff with her daughter, and what happened afterwards didn't matter. "Haven't I lost her anyway?" she asked. "She loves that boy, she calls herself a Muslim, she won't look at me, she cooks her own meals so she doesn't have to eat pork, she prays, she avoids talking to me...Doesn't that mean it's all over?" Alice continued to talk to herself, getting everything out of her system, gearing up to face her daughter as the world she'd so painstakingly constructed over the past twenty years collapsed in front of her eyes.

She was a determined woman, a fighter, and life's problems didn't intimidate her. She'd managed just fine when Pierre left her; she'd brought up Louise without help from anybody. But the way her relationship with Louise was heading disturbed her deeply, which made her hesitate before taking a final decision. It was a battle between heart and mind. On the one hand, she wanted to keep Louise close, to look the other way and keep on going, whatever the cost. On the other hand, she wanted to kick Louise out and get on with life without her, just as she'd done with religion, and with Pierre.

Did a mother's love have to put up with bloody-mindedness, with arrogance? *But isn't this what I deserve for being so open-minded?* Alice wondered. Was she responsible or was she the victim? Where did the truth lie? She was no longer sure. How could she possibly be responsible for her daughter's decisions? Her conviction was growing: it *was* time to have it out with her daughter. She would demolish her arguments; she would prove that her behaviour was the result of bad judgement, of misdirected curiosity, of simple childishness.

Now that her mind was made up, Alice felt relieved, less confused. She could concentrate on her work. As she strode down the hospital corridor she felt a surge of the old energy she had feared she'd lost forever. She completed her morning rounds, took her patients' pulses, jotted down their blood pressure and temperature. Her movements were calm, precise. She always had a smile to spare, a word of encouragement for the sick. The day flashed by.

Alice got ready to go home. She took the bus but got off two stops before hers: she felt like walking. Winter had arrived but the temperature was still relatively mild. She felt upbeat, she felt like gulping in big breaths of fresh air. Snow covered the sides of the road; in some places it had turned black with pollution from the passing cars. She walked ahead with purpose, thinking about the best way to broach the subject with her daughter. She would be straightforward, ask her exactly why she had chosen to become a Muslim. She wouldn't touch on the matter of Ameur. She would not judge her daughter, only listen to her.

Despite the relatively mild temperature, Alice began to shiver. She sped up, and surprised herself by climbing the stairs more quickly than usual. Louise hadn't arrived yet, so she decided to prepare dinner. Ever since Louise had become a Muslim she'd almost turned vegetarian, but occasionally she bought a small quantity of chicken or meat at the Arab market not far from their building.

Alice usually never touched the little packages—it was up to Louise to use them as she wished—but tonight she wanted to demonstrate her goodwill. She removed two pieces of meat from the fridge, washed them, and put them in a saucepan with some spices and a few drops of oil. Then she prepared mashed potatoes with butter, milk, and grated cheese, the way Louise loved them. She had just finished preparing the meal when she heard Louise come in the front door.

Louise greeted her mother and headed for her room. It was time for her to pray. The smell of the meal filled the apartment.

As soon as she had finished praying, Louise went to the kitchen. Alice was seated, awaiting her daughter. Her face showed no emotion.

Louise put on her best, most neutral face. "Thanks for the dinner, Mum," she said in a low voice.

"I used some of the meat you bought," Alice replied.

Louise did not react, but she understood that her mother was trying to tell her something. Seated facing one another, the two began to eat.

"So, you really want to stay a Muslim?" asked Alice, the expression of disappointment on her face masking the beating of her heart.

"Mum, I've found happiness, a reason for living, and now you want me to turn my back on it all?" she replied.

"Are you turning your back on me, on the freedom I brought you up in? Is that it?"

Louise felt sick at the sound of her mother's words. "No, I'll never turn my back on you, Mum. But I've made another choice in life. Please, try to understand me. All I'm turning my back on is my old life . . ." Her eyes filled with tears. She was doing everything she could to control her emotions.

But Alice, cool and contained, went on. "Don't you think you're under the influence of your friend Ameur, that you've lost your ability to judge?"

That was the argument that terrified Louise. She piped up, "Mum, it's true I love Ameur. But I've really chosen to become a Muslim. It's my own choice, not his, believe me."

Alice fell silent and stared straight ahead. She didn't want to look at Louise's emotion-wracked face. She had to leave the table. The two slices of halal meat lay untouched on her plate.

Louise stood up, eyes still moist with tears, and put her arms around her mother, then hugged her. *How long has it been since the last time?* she wondered.

Alice pretended to be unmoved. Was it the feeling of defeat after having tried everything? A few seconds went by.

Louise didn't want to break away. She could smell her

mother's floral perfume. It reminded her of the warmth and peace of her childhood. Everything was always right, everything predictable. Why the conflict, why the constant quarrelling now? *If we could only not talk about religion*, she thought.

Alice let her daughter hug her, and felt once more the warmth of her arms. *If only she would give up Ameur and those wild ideas of his*... she thought.

Both women were holding fast to their positions; neither would give an inch. Only love still held them together. But it was a fragile and delicate link. How much longer could it hold?

Louise kissed her mother's shoulder and then ran off to her room. She had a lump in her throat. Hugging her mother had lifted her spirits, brought her closer to the woman she feared had become her enemy. What must she do now to win back her confidence? She had no idea.

Alice remained seated in the kitchen, lost in thought. The morning's enthusiasm had given way to sleepiness, to a powerful urge to forget, to escape. She looked at the meat that remained on her daughter's plate, picked it up and deposited it on hers, sliced it into smaller pieces and put it in her mouth. It had gone cold. Even with the spices it had no taste; everything about it was insipid.

21

Daddy dearest,

Well, it's New Year's, with all the usual happiness, sadness, and surprises. There's something new at home, though. You must have heard that Mommy hired a lady to give Lynne and Mona private lessons. I think it's a great idea. They were having a lot of trouble in math. They really don't have a choice in the matter—they've got to pass their courses in order to finish high school and get into university. She seems nice enough, but a little sad. But Lynne and Mona say she really knows her stuff. You know how unusual it is for them to like their teachers, so now I'm hoping they can improve their marks and pass their courses.

Nothing new on my side; I'm hoping this semester will be as good, if not better, than the last. For a couple of weeks now it's been snowing steadily, and the whole town is covered with a blanket of white. In fact, the snow hasn't stopped falling. And it hasn't gotten any warmer either!

And how are you doing? I know how busy you are, and that

you can't afford to pay us a visit, but why don't you call me more often? Give it a try! Here I'm beginning to make friends at university. Know what? I joined the Muslim Students Association! And it's not bad at all. There are students from just about everywhere—Pakistanis, Arabs, and even some Canadians who converted to Islam. It's a cool place. And nothing like the closed-minded people you find over there.

I met a Canadian girl who became a Muslim—Louise is her name. She's really nice, and we get along very well. We organize lectures on various topics. That way I feel I'm doing something positive and also I can learn about a different world. I'm anxious to hear your voice. Take care—
Your daughter,

Lama

Lama stifled a yawn; it was time to turn in. She laid the letter down on her night table. Tomorrow she would post it. This session was shaping up to be much harder than the last. She'd signed up for a course in accounting that demanded a lot of effort. But challenges didn't frighten Lama; she'd done well so far and had every intention of keeping up her good work.

Once she began to make friends at university she had felt less pressure to return to Dubai to live. Of course she missed her father—she could barely wait until summer, when he would visit them—but university was a new world for her. It had nothing to do with high school and all the adolescent foolishness that went on there. Was she growing up or was it simply that Lama was ready to break out of the family cocoon and build a different world for herself? Probably both. Lama was no rebel determined at all costs not to identify with her mother. But thanks to her friends, she was learning to recognize another face of Canada.

Lama's efforts to find a foothold, to put down roots, were beginning to pay off. She divided her time between her courses and socializing with her new friends at the Muslim Students Association. Never once did she regret her decision to join, and she attended meetings regularly. She became involved in charitable work and chatted with other members about the stress of exams and the burden of classwork. No longer was she alone, but was surrounded by people just like her. Each one had his or her story to tell; each one was motivated to learn from life.

She thought about Louise, how kind she was, how open-minded. Lama was sure the two of them would become good friends. Nor had it taken her long to figure out that Louise and Ameur were in love. He was always looking in Louise's direction, as if he was afraid of losing her. But Lama had noticed something strange in that young man's eyes. She kept her distance; there was something about him she didn't trust.

22

Over many long nights, Sally thought it through carefully. She visited all the websites she liked and respected. Nothing prohibited her from communicating with a boy by email. She could not see the boy, could not meet him, and therefore could not be attracted to him. She was sure the whole thing was one hundred percent halal.

But Sally hadn't factored in one thing: she was caught in the clutches of a faceless virtual love. She had fallen for the tender words, for verses whispered by fingertips. Most of all, the sense of mystery had bewitched her, tempered her religious zeal and softened her intransigence. She was under the spell of the messages, which kept coming, and was seeking one thousand and one reasons to contact the unknown boy.

Besides, he wasn't entirely unknown to her. For some time he had been signing his messages with an *S*. She suspected even more that it was Sam. Now she was preparing to answer him for the first time.

Hair falling free over her shoulders, she was seated on

the edge of her bed. She wore one of the skirts her mother had bought her, the kind she had refused to wear until now. Her fingers were trembling. Again and again she prayed, "O Allah, protect me from danger!" Then, all at once, as if driven by a strange power, her fingers began to type on the tiny keyboard of her BlackBerry.

In the name of God, the Merciful, the Compassionate. Dear S, I would like to thank you for all the messages you've sent me over the last few weeks. Your words are kind, and I'm really touched. I am ready to make your acquaintance, but on condition that you reveal your full name, and that you are Muslim. If you are ready to reveal your identity, I will continue to communicate with you; if not, this will be the last time I write. Sally.

Her fingers started to tremble again. Before pressing the Send button, she hesitated and reread her short message. The tone and the words she'd chosen seemed right. The message was firm and gentle at the same time. Firm enough to keep bad intentions at arm's length, gentle enough to leave the door ajar.

Sally was proud of herself. By acting this way she had clearly displayed her religious convictions. She was convinced she was behaving correctly and that the sheikhs whom she followed so assiduously would be in complete agreement. She pressed the button. The message was sent.

From far away she heard her mother's voice calling. She stepped out of her room, went down the stairs, and turned towards the kitchen. Fawzia was frying samosas. She had just stuffed them and was now dropping them one after another into a deep pot of hot oil, leaving them to fry long enough to turn a golden brown before removing them.

"Mommy, do you need anything?" Sally asked her mother solicitously.

Fawzia could hardly believe her ears. It had been a long time since her daughter had spoken to her like that. She smiled and looked her in the eyes. She could sense a change in her daughter's attitude. Sally blushed and looked away.

Fawzia pretended not to notice and continued to retrieve samosas from the boiling oil. "Can you get me some more paper towels to absorb the oil?"

Sally did as she was asked without a word. She could feel her mother's inquisitive gaze, and it was as if she knew the whole story about the anonymous messages.

In reality Fawzia knew nothing, but her age and life experience told her that her daughter's behaviour might have something to do with the emergence of new feelings. Could it be a new-found friend? A budding love? Fawzia was determined to find out. She felt deep gratitude to whoever that person might be.

Sally ate a few samosas—they were exquisite. The cumin seeds her mother had mixed into the dough yielded their fragrance in the mouth, mingling with the piquant and pungent taste of ginger. She wiped her mouth on a paper napkin, made sure her mother was still busy frying samosas, went back to her room, and stretched out on her bed.

She contemplated her BlackBerry on the night table. Nothing. No message had popped up in the inbox. The silence worried her, and her heart began to beat faster. What if The Boy Next Door didn't write to her again? What if he hadn't appreciated what she'd written? Remorse swept over her and suddenly she regretted sending the message. But wasn't she satisfied with the words she'd chosen? No longer, for there was no answer. The Boy Next Door, or S, was ignoring her. What if he wanted nothing to do with her? Then what? Sally wondered, devoured by anxiety and fear. What if the whole thing was just a prank?

She considered logging in to one of her favourite online chat groups and talking it over with the other members, but her heart just wasn't in it. She was exhausted, as if she'd just finished a footrace. Every muscle in her body felt stiff and sore. She shut her eyes, but the voices of regret would not stop echoing in her head.

She got to her feet and drew the curtains. She needed rest. It was at that moment that she heard her BlackBerry vibrate. A knife pierced her flesh. She picked up the tiny device and checked the sender's name. FROM: *boy next door.* SUBJECT: *your message.*

She scrolled down. The words lashed her eyes like rain against a windowpane. *In the name of God, the Merciful, the Compassionate. My name is Sam, the boy in your class. I would very much like for us to see each other.*

Sally's head began to spin. Her eyes glazed over. Her temples throbbed. She sat down again on the edge of her bed, let the BlackBerry fall to the floor, closed her eyes, and held her head in her hands.

23

The bus carrying Emma and Sara home was almost empty. Emma was happy; Sara sat close beside her, staring out the window. Soon she would begin tutoring Mrs. Bibi's two girls. It wasn't the idea of earning a bit more money every month that pleased her most, but the fact of being useful, of drawing on her knowledge, of regaining her self-confidence, and above all, of being able to forget her divorce and her loneliness.

She wanted to be an example for her daughter, to be strong, to meet life on its own terms. She didn't want to sink into depression or become a victim. She did not want to return to Tunisia and face the pained expressions of the people she knew. What she wanted very badly was to forget and to find her own way in the world.

Emma was determined to keep hunting for work. Part-time teaching was only a stopgap measure to keep her active. Jobs were not a dime a dozen, and she knew it. Getting an interview would not be easy, but her visit to Mrs. Bibi's had restored her confidence. A sudden onrush of optimism propelled her towards the future.

The bus had reached the stop nearest their home, and Sara tugged at her sleeve. Sara thanked the driver, who responded with a smile. Snow was still falling. At one of the nearby townhouses a woman in her fifties was leaning against her open door, smoking a cigarette and watching the tendrils of smoke drift skywards until they dissipated. She waved to Emma and Sara.

After a moment of hesitation, Emma answered with a timid hello.

The woman addressed them. "Winter's hardly here and already I'm chilled to the bone!"

"I don't much like the long winters either," ventured Emma prudently.

"I don't blame you. We don't see the sun very much...It's depressing...Well, good evening, time to get back inside." The woman stubbed out her cigarette in an empty can that stood on the windowsill, then closed the door behind her.

Emma stepped inside her own house. Everything was still. She went upstairs with Sara to get her ready for bed.

Sara wanted a bedtime story. She put on her pyjamas, brushed her teeth, and lay down on her mattress to wait for her mother. Emma's mind was far away, but Sara's insistent gaze brought her back to reality. She pulled a book from the pile and began to read.

Ten minutes later Sara had fallen asleep, exhausted by the visit to Mrs. Bibi's and the long bus ride there and back. Emma switched off the light, turned on the nightlight, and retired to her bedroom. She was not sleepy.

Images from the past few years flashed before her eyes. In front of Sara she wanted to appear happy and strong, but when she was alone, the velvet gloves slipped off and the mask fell away. She became vulnerable again. What could she possibly hide? She was naked, with nothing to protect her from others. Her feelings, her fears, her unhappiness lay exposed.

She wanted to weep but no tears came to relieve her. All at once she felt too weak to keep up the daily battle. Her whole body shivered as though a deep chill had burrowed its way insidiously down to her bones. She thought back to her childhood, to her mother's enveloping arms, to her father's tender affection. She remembered the spring sunlight that brought her so much happiness as she chased the neighbour's cat through the family garden. The gentle warmth of her happy memories seemed to wash over her.

She laid her head on the pillow and a faint smile crept across her face. She kept her eyes open in the darkness. All that had gone before would help her face the present unafraid. A feathery sensation tickled her eyelids; tears filled her eyes and ran unhindered down her cheeks. Hurt gave way to relief. How Emma wished that the feeling would never leave her.

24

Unblinking, Louise's wide blue eyes travelled back and forth across Ameur's face. She was on the verge of tears but was doing everything she could to hold them back. Ameur's words flowed like a rushing brook, rising in her ears. Those same words that for months had caused her to dream — it was the way he spoke that had seduced her — that had brought her to Islam and transformed her into another person, were now inflicting pain. Ameur was speaking of his mother, and how deeply hurtful their relationship was to her, how he hoped to see her health restored, to be at peace with her.

No sooner had she learned that her son intended to marry Louise than Fatma took to her bed, unable to rouse herself. She could not approve of her son's marriage to a Canadian girl. She wanted Ameur to marry her niece Iman, a well-brought-up Egyptian who'd attended the American University in Cairo. She would be compatible with her son.

Face pallid, lips trembling, Ameur attempted to explain. "I

must obey my mother. I can't just stand by while her health suffers on account of me..."

How Louise wished right then that her own mother was next to her. Despite the coldness that had come between them, she had only one thought: to nestle in her arms, to escape Ameur's gaze.

"The choice is a hard one for me, Louise. You have to understand. There's no other way."

Louise wanted to vent her anger, her fury right in Ameur's face. She wanted to tell him she thought he was a coward. She couldn't believe he would drop her, especially after she had changed her entire life for him. She was unable to fathom why he could not convince his mother of his love for her. But she simply picked up her backpack and got to her feet.

Ameur wanted to hold her back. He implored her, but she would stay not a moment longer. He watched as the girl with blue eyes disappeared. His dream had turned to dust. Fatma, his mother, had other dreams for him. He had no choice but to submit; he could not rebel against her. He was a captive of the inevitable.

Louise made her way through the corridors of the university as if on automatic pilot. She wanted to get outside, into the sun. She hoped to find comfort in the clear skies of this early spring day. Maybe then she would feel better and could think clearly about her future. What could she hope for after what she'd just heard? How would she ride out the storm?

Snow still lay in mounds on the sidewalk. Smaller heaps melted indolently under the fierce rays of spring sunlight. Water flowed in tiny rivulets that joined, then divided into several smaller streams. Louise walked staring straight ahead, looking at no one. She could see only Ameur's mouth, his body language, the way he raised his eyebrows. His words darted back and forth in her head like autumn leaves that could not decide where to alight.

She wanted to forget, to shut her eyes, to forget Ameur and that adventure that had carried her so far from home. She had always felt so confident, so happy at finding both a man to love and a faith to guide her in life. And now that man had rejected her in order to obey his mother and to ingratiate himself in her eyes.

Louise had never felt so miserable before. She walked along, crossing one street after another, hands thrust deep into the pockets of her green windbreaker, strands of hair hanging down on her forehead, staring off into the distance. A feeling of shame swept over her—a feeling she'd never known before. Shame at her own arrogance, at the way she had mistreated her mother. She wanted to scrub Ameur's face from her memory, but his clear, bell-like voice, his charm, and his eloquence kept returning, haunting her. Her body was the victim, her mind the executioner. She wanted to shriek, to lash out, to flee, to break his hold on her—all in vain. The executioner was too strong, impregnable, pitiless. Her mind would give her no peace.

Unconsciously Louise had found her way home. She slipped into the apartment. The sight of the furniture, the paintings on the walls, the bibelots arranged on small tables, all reminded her of reality. In them she could feel her mother's organization and devotion, and she felt secure. She went into her room, the little room that as recently as yesterday she thought she would be leaving for good. Ameur's words this morning had brought her back to earth, shattered the beautiful plans she had been making for months on end. Her bed was meticulously made. Her white desk was in perfect order.

On her night table lay a copy of the Qur'an. From it she would ardently read an extract every evening before going to sleep. She felt a twinge in her heart. Her prayer rug was folded up beside her chair. She looked at it with bitterness. Ameur had given it to her the day she became a Muslim. It was a handsome red carpet, interwoven with gold thread in geometric motifs that reminded her of a bed of tulips in the centre of a garden. She unrolled it and knelt down. But she no longer knew what to do; it was as though she had forgotten all the prayers she once knew by heart. Sobbing overcame her. Body shaking, she bent forward, her forehead touching the ground, and murmured, "My God, I am lost. Guide me, for I do not know what to do..."

25

Sally had been right. She'd sensed it from the start, and today she had proof, right on her BlackBerry. Sam had lifted the veil that concealed his identity. He'd greeted her as a Muslim. He wanted to meet her! How had Sally, the cautious girl, the one who wore the niqab, who took religion so seriously, come to this? "But what did I do wrong? What did I do that was *haram*? Absolutely nothing," she whispered, as if in her own defence. "I didn't speak to him, didn't shake his hand. I only read his poems, and answered his messages only once and no more."

Sally was caught in her own trap, like a spider captured in its web. And like a captured spider, she struggled to escape. Her first reaction was to answer Sam's request with a no, but she hesitated. How could she have let things develop so far, only to destroy them at one blow, as she was about to do? "I have to think this through," she said to herself.

She was apprehensive and at the same time felt the call of adventure. She couldn't retreat. How could she erase from her memory all those messages she'd received from The Boy Next Door? She'd read them time and time again. She could not deny the impact of his words on her, on her emotions, on her relationship with her parents. Even though their connection was a strictly virtual one, it had become vital for her.

Sally was not prepared to bring it to an end. For if Sam loved her, why not meet him, become acquainted with him, perhaps even — who knows? — marry him. She blushed at the thought of a face-to-face meeting, but just as quickly promised to behave according to God's law, which reassured her. In evoking His name Sally felt stronger, better prepared to deal with any eventuality. Her faith would guide her, of that she was convinced.

This time she decided not to answer Sam before she talked it over with her mother. At first the very idea seemed foolish, considering her mother's laxity in religious matters, but rapidly it began to appeal to her. What an excellent way to rebuild bridges between her and her parents.

Her mind made up, she stood to pray. The need to thank God for guiding her onto the right path overwhelmed her. Her prayer completed, she was surprised to find herself hoping that her encounter with Sam might lead to marriage...

Fawzia was in the small room she had transformed into a sewing workshop, putting the finishing touches on an orange tunic. The finely woven fabric slid through the sewing machine and slipped through her fingers as though attempting to escape its fate. The tunic was destined for one of Fawzia's friends; it would be ready in a few days time, she had promised. She was in a fine mood, humming the refrain of a popular song. Ever since her daughter had become so affectionate again with her and her husband, Fawzia had returned to her old routines and reawakened to life.

Needless to say, Sally wasn't ready to abandon the niqab, but for Fawzia it was no longer the end of the world that she'd feared when it all began. She had become accustomed to seeing her daughter dressed that way. Gradually, beneath the frightening long black sack dresses, she had rediscovered the daughter she had known before. Fawzia was waiting patiently for the day when she would discover the secret behind the change in Sally.

She was startled to see her daughter standing in front of her. Fawzia had not been expecting a heart-to-heart talk, but Sally's eyes were so filled with emotion that she understood this moment would be decisive. With a sudden movement, she lifted her foot from the pedal. The orange fabric slipped to the floor. Fawzia, hardly noticing it, smiled at her daughter and said, "What is it, Sally? Is something on your mind?"

Sally knew her mother was good at putting people around her at ease, but she hadn't realized how truly skilful she was. She pulled up a stool, sat down, and said, "There's this boy who's been sending me messages on my BlackBerry for some time. Up until yesterday I didn't answer him, and now he says he wants to meet me. Sam is his name; he's in my class. He got my email address from one of my friends. I hardly know him..."

In an effort not to give the wrong impression, she hurriedly added, "But I swear I've never spoken to him. Only one message, the one I sent yesterday."

Fawzia was stunned. She knit her brows as she attempted to digest all this information at once. For a split second Sally feared she'd made a terrible mistake by confiding in her mother; she didn't know what to think.

Fawzia bent over and picked up the piece of orange fabric from the floor. She smiled. The mystery was solved. Sam was the one who had returned her Sally to her. She had to meet him. Looking at her daughter, she said, "He's in your class, you say? What does he look like? Is he a good boy?"

Sally blushed. "I don't know, I never looked straight at him. He always sits at the back of the lecture hall. Anyway, he looks nice . . . or at least normal . . ."

It was clear to Fawzia that Sally was already interested in this boy. "You may invite him to our house. I'll speak to your father."

Sally could hardly believe her ears. She opened her mouth, but no sound came out.

26

"Did you ever think of working in an Arab country?" Mrs. Bibi asked Emma one day, out of the blue.

Emma didn't know what to say. She was putting on her coat; Sara was already waiting at the door. Was Mrs. Bibi serious or did she want to share something that had popped up at one of her morning get-togethers with her circle of friends?

The weekly two-hour tutoring session had just ended. Emma's two pupils were showing signs of progress and she was doing everything she could to bring them up to speed. The girls had fallen well behind. There was no way she could repair the damage done over the past few years in mere months, but it was apparent that her two charges were responding to her prodding and making a greater effort to solve the problems. There was still a lot of work to be done.

Emma stared at Mrs. Bibi, incredulous.

"I swear on my daughters' heads, my question is serious..." Mrs. Bibi continued, straightening her skirt, which showed her knees, and brushing a wisp of hair from her forehead.

"To tell you the truth, I've never thought about it," Emma answered.

"Well, start thinking about it. If you're interested, I've got a fabulous idea for you!"

"What do you mean?" Emma exclaimed. "What country are you thinking of? Not Tunisia, I hope!"

Mrs. Bibi looked upset. "Of course not! What I mean is... a rich country, a place with a lot of opportunity, good pay, good shopping, everything you need...you know what I'm saying?"

Emma stood there gaping. Mrs. Bibi wanted to find her a job in Dubai or another Gulf country?

Suddenly Mrs. Bibi looked tired, exasperated.

"You know what, we'll talk it over another time. Bye-bye, my dear. But think it over—I'm very serious."

Emma slipped on her shoes and left the house with Sara in tow. Mrs. Bibi had said all she was going to say for the moment. Emma remained silent for most of the bus ride, and Sara too. But as the two drew closer to home, Sara piped up. "Mummy, where are the Gulf countries? In Mexico?"

It was all Emma could do not to burst out laughing. "No, sweetie, farther than Mexico. Closer to Saudi Arabia, where Muslims go for the pilgrimage. Understand?"

Sara was perplexed. "Why does Mrs. Bibi want you to go so far away to work? And me, where will I stay?"

Emma hugged her daughter and said, "Don't worry, darling, I'll always be with you. It's all talk. We'll see what happens."

Apparently reassured, Sara didn't mention the idea again.

But Emma could not forget any of what Mrs. Bibi had said. That night she tossed and turned in her bed as she replayed Mrs. Bibi's words in her mind. *What did she mean? Why is she making such a suggestion now? Why does she want to help me when she's known me for only a few months? What if Mrs. Bibi has actually found me a job in one of the Gulf States? Would I be prepared for the adventure? And just what kind of work could I do over there in any case?*

Emma slept very badly that night. How she wished that Mrs. Bibi had never mentioned the idea. Now she would have to wait an entire week to find out what came next. She barely knew whether she was awake or asleep. First she saw herself lost in a desert, then in a blizzard: blazing heat followed by intense cold. She shivered, and felt as though she were drenched with sweat.

In the morning she thought about speaking with her mother. Mrs. Bibi's proposition had thrown her into confusion, and the sound of her mother's voice would help her sort things out. But she held back; her mother was ill, and she did not want to disturb her.

The sound of knocking at the door made her jump, rousing her from her torpor. The knocks were faint but insistent. She didn't know anyone in the neighbourhood, so she was afraid to answer. She peered out her kitchen window but could not make out the person. She decided to pretend not to hear the knocks as they tapped out their cadence on the door.

But what if it's someone from the city to do maintenance work? What if it's urgent? she thought. She turned the key and cracked open the door. There in front of her stood the woman she'd seen a few weeks ago smoking a cigarette on her front porch.

In her arms she was holding a baby; the child's curly hair fell across her forehead, and she had a plump face and an impish air. Emma vaguely recognized the little girl, but couldn't recall where she might have seen her.

She felt relieved and opened the door wide, no longer afraid.

The woman smiled. "Hi, it's me. My name is Jeanne and I live in the house at the end of the row. And this is Melanie. I've got another daughter—she's in school right now—her name is Cathy." Jeanne stopped for a moment to clear her throat and then continued, "Anyway, look—I'm a little embarrassed—do you have some matches or maybe a lighter? I've lost mine and can't find it, and I really need a smoke."

Emma hardly knew what to say. She looked her visitor over. The woman was dressed on a budget. She had a thin face, yellowed teeth, and searching eyes, but a happy look and, most of all, that adorable baby in her arms. Then, all at once, Emma made the connection—the little girl who'd spoken to her a few months ago, just before she moved into the neighbourhood, had been carrying the same baby on her hip.

Emma said, "I think I've already met your older daughter, when I was in the neighbourhood for the first time, before I moved in. She asked me where I was going to live."

"That's Cathy! What a busybody!" exclaimed Jeanne with a laugh. "She always wants to find out everything about her neighbours. . . . But she's a good girl, she really helps me out a lot, looking after her little sister when I'm too tired. . ." As though Jeanne's body sought to confirm her words, a violent bout of coughing swept over her, contorting her features.

For the first time in years Emma was overcome with pity

for someone other than herself. "Well, come in then," she said. "My name is Emma and I've got a daughter named Sara. Come in and let me see if I've got some matches to spare."

27

The storm over, Louise awoke to a new reality. She looked closely at the wreckage left by her abrupt break with Ameur. She wanted neither to see him or speak to him. Disgust had taken the place of love. How naive she had been!

How could he have dropped her at his mother's whim? How could he have forgotten his promises? It was betrayal, wasn't it, a lie! Wasn't he the one who constantly reminded her of the importance of good behaviour, of the need for a proper understanding of religion. Didn't he realize he was at fault? He had outright lied, had misled her! If he felt too weak to confront his mother, why did he even bother with her in the first place? Why build an entire relationship based on some faint hope?

Louise was as furious with herself as she was with Ameur. How immature she felt, how incapable of making the right choice. *What if Mum is right? Maybe I am nothing but a numb-skull, someone who'se been brainwashed,* she thought. *If I'd never met Ameur I would never have become a Muslim, and I wouldn't be so unhappy today!* Louise could only look on as the stable, coherent world she'd constructed collapsed before her very eyes. Ameur had bewitched her, and had dragged her into a labyrinth from which she could not escape.

Alone with her thoughts, she was terrified of telling her mother that Ameur had dropped her for a cousin. That kind of ending to the story would only confirm Alice's predictions. Louise could already hear her saying, *See, if you'd only listened to me none of this would have happened.* And that was the last thing she wanted to hear. Deep down, she knew her mother would not turn her back on her, but she was not yet ready to face those reproachful eyes.

She wanted someone to talk to, someone who would understand and would not judge. That person's name had to be Lama. The two of them got along very well, so why not confide in her? Lama was in the best possible position to help — she came from the same culture as Ameur but had grown up here, in Canada, which put her between the two worlds. She could see things from another point of view. And Lama had a critical mind, Louise had noticed at meetings of the student association. Lama was just the person she needed.

The two girls met in the university cafeteria, a noisy place crowded with students of every size and shape. Some ate while they read the newspaper, while others congregated to chat and laugh boisterously. There were solitary ones and ones who hung out in groups, all of them gathered in the same huge dining room. Lama and Louise found a table off to the side and sat down facing each other.

Louise spoke first. "Lama, I look on you as a special friend, and that's why I asked to see you. You know I became a

Muslim a few months ago, and that I was getting ready to marry Ameur…but now it's all off. Two days ago he told me that his parents, primarily his mother, don't want him to have anything to do with me. They prefer that he marry one of his cousins in Egypt…" She blushed and her voice quavered.

Lama listened attentively, heart throbbing, as Dina's face during the wedding ceremony flashed across her mind.

"I feel like Ameur has betrayed me with his words and promises. I can't understand why he's acting this way, and worst of all, I can feel my faith wavering—I who was so strong. Well, I'm finding out just how vulnerable I can be, and how easily someone could change my life."

Anger at Ameur swept over Lama. Could this be the reason for the mistrust she'd always felt towards him? Maybe Ameur's gentleness concealed a weak personality; maybe he was caught between tradition and modern life, trapped by a desire to please everybody at the risk of losing everything. That was exactly what Lama had always criticized so sharply. She was against her mother's hypocrisy, against her sisters' egotistical, self-interested obedience, against their community's superficial attachment to its dusty archaic principles in the name of religion while at the same time lies, backbiting, and envy were everywhere.

She looked Louise in the eye. "You're not the only one who's furious with Ameur. I've been banging my head against that wall for years. Ameur is one of those guys who want to be stronger than tradition. He played with fire like a little boy playing with matches, but his mother was quick to call him to order and crack down. He thought his education and his intelligence would make him invulnerable, but reality caught up with him. Louise, you've just discovered one aspect of the problems I run into every day. I understand exactly how hurt you are. If you want to know the truth, I'm glad it happened now—at least that way you'll be vaccinated."

A faint smile played across Louise's face but almost immediately turned to a frown. "When I became a Muslim, I thought I was giving meaning to my life. I thought I was freeing myself from domination of all kinds. It looks like I misunderstood everything. I just don't know what to think anymore..."

Lama nodded sympathetically. "I'm warning you, it's only the beginning."

They stayed there for hours, talking it out. Louise's eyes glistened with tears, but her heart felt lighter. There was revolt in Lama's voice, but also happiness at finding a friend who was also in search of the truth.

28

Samia Bibi hadn't been joking when she asked Emma about working in an Arab country. Besides, she wasn't the type to joke. She searched for happiness in the nice things, the pleasant things in life: a beautiful dress, a cigarette, expensive sheets, top-quality clothing for her daughters, good-humoured friends who enjoyed a fine cup of Turkish coffee flavoured with cardamom. From the day she had met Emma she'd read the sadness in her features, recognized the signs of misfortune in her eyes. In Emma's face she saw something of herself, as if in a bright, sharply focused photograph that reminded her of her own misfortune. And that imagined photo had bothered Samia. There was more than kindness in her concern for Emma; she was acting to protect her own happiness. She wanted to replace Emma's image with something better, one with the smile of a TV personality, a shining face surrounded by sparkling stars. But she didn't know quite how to begin. First she had to learn more about her life, about the reasons for her sadness.

During their conversations, Mrs. Bibi had taken note of Emma's separation from her husband, the distance that separated her from her mother, her solitude and humiliation, not to mention the unemployment and poverty that had become her lot. Mrs. Bibi understood that she could not repair Emma's relationship with her former husband, nor could she convince her to return to live with her ageing mother, but she was certain she could find work for Emma with her husband's business in Dubai. After all, Emma was an educated woman who spoke English, French, and Arabic; she could certainly find an opening in a country with a constant need for qualified manpower. Not to mention that Emma was Muslim, so she would quickly become accustomed to life in the Emirates.

The only weaknesses in her plan were how she would convince her husband to hire Emma, and how Emma, the beneficiary, would react to the suggestion. But dwelling on the negatives would have been to ignore Mrs. Bibi's determination and perseverance when it came to the search for happiness. All she needed was a good strategy and a little time for her plan to come to fruition. Before talking with her husband in Dubai, she concluded that it was necessary to convince Emma to accept the idea of leaving Canada. She would have to make the prospect of working in Dubai an attractive one, persuade her to use her abilities rather than stay in Ottawa and live on her meagre monthly welfare stipend. That wouldn't be hard for Mrs. Bibi. She knew Dubai well, and the attractions and drawbacks of living there. She would paint Emma the most glowing possible portrait of the city.

The idea brought a smile to her face. She glanced over towards the kitchen. The floor shone; the double refrigerator she'd just bought was bursting with provisions; high-priced china and silverware filled the cupboards. So much space! What a striking contrast to the tiny house where she and her three daughters had once lived, suffocating in the heat. Immense traffic jams every morning, and no sooner did they end than they would begin again when the offices and shops closed for the day.

But what had irritated her most was the quality of the Arab women whose company she kept—that was the reason she had no intention of returning. Those women, who came from everywhere, were too superficial for her; they completely lacked class and dreamed only of making money and returning to their own country to build a house. Mrs. Bibi felt that she herself was above such wretched considerations. She was searching for joie de vivre, for fine food and beautiful objects, and very occasionally she would read a book in English to remind herself that she had once studied English literature. In Canada she had found women of another kind to help her forget her solitude—women more accustomed to Western culture, women who appreciated the value of the things they bought, women who knew how to stroke her vanity. Those were the principle reasons why she did not want to live in Dubai.

But for Emma things would be completely different. She could find work in her field, could be appreciated for what she was and for what she could do. She could enjoy life to the fullest, meet other people and escape from the isolation that seemed to be engulfing her more with every passing day. Helping others in their lives was Mrs. Bibi's way of coming to terms with her own life, of giving it meaning.

Those were the ideas that filled her mind as she focused on the eggplant purée she was preparing. After emptying it into a shallow bowl, she finely chopped some sprigs of parsley as a garnish and dribbled a few drops of olive oil over the mixture. Then temptation overcame her. She dipped her finger into the bowl, pulled it out, and licked it. Her eyes gleamed—she was satisfied with her work.

The ringing of the telephone interrupted her train of thought. "Ah, Leila, it's you. I was just about to call. In fact, I wanted to talk to you about Suzie's dress. What a disaster! She looked like a sack of potatoes. I saw it yesterday, at the reception at her place . . ."

29

Sam was expected at the Husseins'. He'd accepted the invitation Sally sent him by way of an answer. Sally was happy that at last she would meet The Boy Next Door, the one who had captured her attention, her BlackBerry, and her heart.

Without even knowing him, Sally felt that she had loved this young man for months. She wanted to know everything about him, and most of all, why he was interested in a girl like her. The other question that intrigued her was whether he really was a Muslim. In his message he used the Islamic form of greeting, but was it simply out of respect, a way of getting closer to her, or was it out of conviction?

For Sally, everything was clear-cut. Either Sam was a Muslim and she was prepared to get to know him better and even to marry him, or he was an impostor, in which case she would have to forget the whole sorry episode and never speak of it again. One thing was certain: she would marry no one but a Muslim, and not just any Muslim but a real Muslim— one who prayed five times a day, went to the mosque, and wore a beard. At the thought of the beard, she hesitated. Sam did not have a beard. She made up her mind that once she had a good idea of his intentions and his convictions, she would ask him to grow one.

Sally's parents were happy too. Above all, they wanted to ascertain the lad's true intentions, to find out if he was a good boy, polite and well educated. For them the question of religious practice could come later. "The foundations have to be solid. All the rest is secondary..." Ali kept repeating as he turned over in his mind the idea that his daughter might soon be married.

Fawzia could think only of the festivities to come. For the occasion she would prepare a veritable feast: biryani, a dish made of chicken and rice, tiny bouquets of deep-fried breaded cauliflower flavoured with coriander, lentils in a spicy sauce with morsels of lamb, a green salad, and little semolina cakes in a light syrup flavoured with cinnamon and cardamom.

Sam arrived right on time, and Ali greeted him at the door. He was a tall, slender young man with sad eyes. He was simply dressed, with worn running shoes on his feet. The two men barely looked at one another. Sam dared only raise his eyes furtively to glance at Mr. Hussein. Sally's father felt awkward as well. Smiling to mask his embarrassment, he invited the visitor to follow him to the living room.

The contrast between the two was stark, almost comical. Sam, skinny, frail-looking, and reserved, towered over Mr. Hussein, a short, stocky, jovial man who masked his nervousness with a series of jokes that only he laughed at, spoke of his birthplace, and made comments on politics mingled with the latest National Hockey League results. Despite Ali's accent

Sam did his best to follow. He managed to pick up the odd word, smiling occasionally but not daring to speak.

Mrs. Hussein entered the living room, followed by Sally. Fawzia was wearing a vibrantly coloured traditional dress, a muslin shawl barely concealing her hair, and her eyes sparkled. Sally was dressed as usual except that the veil covering her face was white—her mother had insisted so strongly that finally Sally had given in. She stood close to her mother, not even daring to look at Sam. Fawzia, with her exuberant personality and her relaxed and poised manner, helped lighten the atmosphere of the meeting. Everything seemed to have been waiting for her so that the real discussion could begin.

Fawzia placed a platter of fruit on the table and handed Sam a small saucer. He thanked her and immediately served himself. Then she passed saucers to her husband and daughter.

"Sally, would you please bring us the pineapple juice, the water, and the ice cubes? I left them on the kitchen counter."

Sally left the room and Fawzia began. "Mr. Sam, we are very happy to see you. Sally told us that you wanted to meet her, and we are delighted. So, you are in the same class as Sally?"

"Thank you for your invitation. My mother is Canadian, my father from Saudi Arabia. My parents divorced when I was three years old, and I've lived here ever since with my mother. This is my last year at university. For a long time I didn't consider myself a Muslim, but in the last few years I've begun to take an interest in my Arab heritage. I discovered the Muslim faith and accepted it. Sally and I attend the same lecture, and I have nothing but admiration for her fervour and her piety, and that's why I wanted to meet her."

Sally had returned to the room carrying a tray. She listened to Sam attentively, and his poems rushed back into her mind, touching her deeply. Fawzia was in seventh heaven—this lad had surprised her. Could he be the gift of heaven she'd implored for her daughter?

Then all at once, Mr. Ali stood up and broke his silence. "And why not continue this interesting discussion in the dining room?"

Off they went, as if they'd already formed a family. The savoury meal that Fawzia had prepared awaited them.

30

Louise gradually forgot her adventure with Ameur as she grew closer to Lama. The two became inseparable. In Lama Louise had found not only a friend but also a confidante, someone she could turn to in need. And Lama slowly forgot her conflict with her mother. She had discovered in Louise a modern, independent young woman who understood her religion not by way of tradition but as a spiritual search for a more balanced life.

The two would meet regularly after classes. They talked about their studies, their professors, their plans for the future, and about their problems. Their friendship helped them come to terms with their mothers, with their heritage, with their immediate circle. Louise spoke of Ameur but no longer wept. In her faith and in her friendship with Lama, she found the courage to overcome her grief. Her relations with her mother gradually improved; Louise no longer saw Alice as an obstacle to her religious beliefs, and rediscovered her support and love.

To avoid seeing Ameur, she had stopped attending meetings

of the Muslim Students Association. He would only remind her of how naive she had been, how vulnerable. Louise was grateful to him for having brought her to her new religion, but she resented him for his weakness and cowardice. She could not forgive him for having dropped her in the name of tradition and custom. His appearance, his face, his honeyed words, his advice to her—all had combined to convince her that he was the ideal man, the perfect balance between material life and her new spiritual identity as a Muslim. But her budding love had blinded her: she did not notice how the weight of tradition had caused Ameur's spine to bend.

Lama did her best to explain to Louise that Ameur's change of heart was the result of something too powerful to resist, something few people could withstand. "It can happen with marriage, with the birth of a child, or the death of a dear one. We go back to the beginning," she explained, looking Louise straight in the eye as if to convince her of the validity of her theory.

Louise fell silent for an instant, then replied, "Do you think I'll also have a 'back to the beginning' moment? After all, I've rejected everything my mother taught me. Do you think I'll be like her one day?" She smiled sadly, her questioning gaze awaiting Lama's reply.

Her friend answered without missing a beat. "That's a good question, but only time will tell. For the time being, just drink tap water and let everybody else drink from the spring."

The two girls burst out laughing. They were seated on a bench in a small garden at the centre of the campus. A halo of fresh green leaves barely covered most of the trees. Spring was settling in and the sun's rays had shaken them from their winter inertia, flooding them with comforting warmth. As they were chatting and laughing, a girl wearing a niqab strode by briskly. Lama and Louise looked at each other and fell into an embarrassed silence.

Louise was first to break it. "Are you ready to dress that way?"

Lama shrugged. "Not on your life. I can't even bring myself to wear a headscarf, so it's not likely you'd ever see me wearing a niqab. Nope, it's just not my style," she said, with an angry edge to her voice. "What about you?"

Louise sighed. "At one point I was toying with the idea of wearing a headscarf, but I just couldn't do it. I wanted to be a good Muslim, wanted to feel secure...but I wasn't ready, it wasn't a step I was prepared to take. Maybe one day. But the niqab? No...I don't understand it. I have plenty of reservations on the subject, and mostly plenty of questions."

For Lama the niqab symbolized discrimination against women. "Look, with it on you can't work, you can't go out to eat...you're not free, period. It's a way of dressing that comes from certain particular regions, but when you get right down to it, it's still the weight of tradition that holds us back."

Louise seemed a bit less intransigent. "Did you see the girl who just went by? I think she's a student here. Wouldn't that prove that she's like us, that she can study and maybe even find work one day? It's her choice, after all. Shouldn't we try to understand her?"

Lama was losing patience. "Okay, I respect her choice, but I can't understand it. Never, never would I dress like that," she repeated, as if to convince herself once and for all.

To break the tension, Louise joked, "And if you decide at

some point to return to the spring for a drink, will you put on your veil?"

Lama shook her head with a laugh. "My theory only applies to other people. Me, I've been vaccinated."

31

Emma was becoming accustomed to Mrs. Bibi's idea. It came up every time they met. And it wasn't a simple idea any longer; it had become a project. A project that had now taken on concrete form with one of Mr. Bibi's companies, in the shape of a formal application and a possible hiring date. Mrs. Bibi was jubilant; everything was turning out exactly as she had planned.

Ezz Bibi, who normally mistrusted his wife's suggestions, found the idea attractive. The problem with most of her ideas was that they involved substantial expenditure, but this time that was not the case. Samia truly wanted to assist this woman by finding her work and improving her situation. And the suggestion had come at exactly the right time. One of the employees of a company belonging to Mr. Bibi had returned to Egypt to look after his ailing mother; a replacement had to be found. Ever cautious, Mr. Bibi had been taking all the time he needed to find the best candidate, and he hadn't found anyone so far. He asked for more information about Emma.

Emma's feelings went from incredulity to curiosity and from interest to hope. She told her mother, who was happy that her daughter would be closer to her, geographically speaking, and that she would have a job worthy of her university diplomas.

As she prepared her cv, Emma was startled by what she'd accomplished. Ever since her separation she had turned inward, had forgotten who she was in professional terms. But the prospect of moving to Dubai brought her back down to earth and reminded her that life must go on. Sara could feel the change in her mother: she was more optimistic, and most of all, she laughed more often. Both of them were preparing themselves mentally for a departure that looked more and more plausible every day.

Emma did everything she could to convince herself that there was no difference between Canada and Dubai, and that Dubai would be better for her and her daughter. Her job there would make it possible for her to buy a car, to live in an attractive modern apartment, and even to return to Canada for visits. All she'd heard about the exploitation of foreign workers, about racism towards people of certain nationalities, about corruption and the absence of democracy didn't bother her terribly. She wasn't out to change the world, she told herself; rather, she was looking for was a comfortable, peaceful life, a place to bring up her daughter and to forget all she'd been through.

As she gradually drew further away from everything that bound her to Canada, Emma felt at peace with herself. It was a long and trying exercise — after all, she had spent many years here. Everything seemed to be pulling her back: her daughter

Sara, her failed marriage, her lengthy and laborious studies. Everything called out, loud and clear, that this was the country where she belonged. So to break the hold Canada had on her, she began to think only of Dubai. She visualized herself in that cosmopolitan city, going to work every day, winning the respect of her colleagues, driving her daughter to a private school, visiting the shopping centres, going to the beach with Sara, making friends. Now it was a matter of waiting for her contract and her visa.

She knocked on her friend Jeanne's door. Ever since the episode with the matches, the two women had come to know one another better, and it was a friendship that proved beneficial to both. They could not have been more different in character: one was an extrovert, the other an introvert. One had learned to live her life by overcoming misfortune; the other was still torn between past and present. They had both learned from their misadventures and supported one another.

Jeanne suffered from asthma and had reared her two daughters alone. Her first husband had beaten her. At the time she was so ashamed that she didn't say a word to anyone and suffered in silence. But one day she had had enough, and she walked out with her daughter. She never saw her husband again. A few years later she met another man, a "real gentleman," as Jeanne liked to describe him when she told Emma the story. He was well-mannered and treated her and her daughter well. So Jeanne decided to rebuild her life with him, and she gave birth to a second daughter. But this "gentleman" had one shortcoming: he didn't like to work. He slept during the day and spent the night carousing. The breaking point was not long in coming. Jeanne had shown her second husband the door. The two girls paid a high price, but Jeanne did her best to bring them up well.

Emma adored Jeanne's ability to laugh at her own misfortunes, to look them up and down and not to view them as the end of the world. Emma's patience impressed Jeanne, who hoped that one day she could develop such patience herself. The two women spent hours in conversation while Sara and Jeanne's two daughters played together. Everyone forgot their hardships. All that counted was the happiness of the moment.

32

Today Mrs. Bibi positively glittered. She wore a black dress embroidered with tiny semi-precious stones that she'd bought some time ago but had never worn. In truth, Mrs. Bibi was always beautifully dressed and perfectly groomed, but on this occasion her elegance had risen by a notch. Why? She had won her wager and was intent on displaying the fact to everyone, beginning with Emma, the prime subject. Her intention was to proclaim the good news herself—Emma was now officially hired as a computer expert in Mr. Ezz Bibi's firm. What had begun as a caprice was a reality, and what a reality it was!

She was proud of herself and proud of her handiwork, born of her compassion for Emma. For the first time in her life she had contrived to bring happiness to someone else at the same time as herself. It was a new kind of happiness, not the self-centred pleasure of buying fine things and dressing in the latest, most expensive fashions. She awaited Emma's arrival impatiently.

That day Emma decided to leave Sara to play at Jeanne's

house while she went to Mrs. Bibi's for her tutoring session.

Lynne and Mona were making good progress. Their marks had steadily improved. At first they didn't really trust Emma; in fact, they had underestimated her. Behind her back they made fun of the way she dressed, of the slightly lost expression on her face. But as time passed the two girls had to admit that they understood math better, that certain concepts were clearer, and that they could actually solve mathematical problems. So gradually Lynne and Mona had changed their attitude, stopped their childish behaviour, and begun to look on their tutor with respect, even with admiration. The idea that Emma might not be there next year to help them with their math worried them.

Emma paused in front of the Bibi house. The signs of spring were visible everywhere. The grass was still yellow but it was slowly recovering after the recent disappearance of the snow. The bare-branched trees were displaying their first buds, which stood upright in defiance of the cold and ice. An air of renewal permeated the atmosphere, driving away the smell of winter's accumulation of rot and refuse.

Emma rang the doorbell and Mrs. Bibi opened, a broad smile on her face. In comparison with Samia's elegant dress, Emma's clothes make her look like a cleaning lady, but she let nothing show. She looked around for her two pupils.

Mrs. Bibi announced, "You can begin a bit later today. The girls can wait."

Her hostess led her towards the small reception room. Emma thought back to her first visit and how badly she had wanted the tutoring job. Today things were different. The job she wanted was not tutoring the girls but the one Mrs. Bibi had promised her, in Dubai. Emma was concerned. Why did Mrs. Bibi want to talk to her?

She didn't say a word. Her stomach was churning, but she breathed deeply to conceal her apprehension. She repeated silently, as if to reassure herself, *Well, if I'm not accepted over there, I'll still have a roof over my head and food to put on my table. It's not the end of the world.*

The tiny Swarovski crystals on Mrs. Bibi's dress all but dazzled Emma. They drew her eyes to them as they reflected glints of light back onto the walls, the pattern of reflections shifting with Samia's every movement. Octagons replaced hexagons and then vanished in a wild whirl, lending force to the festive look in her eyes. Radiant, she gestured to Emma to take a seat.

"I've got good news for you. My husband tells me that in a few days you'll be getting an official answer to your application for a job in his company."

Emma pinched herself. She wanted to shout for joy, but no sound came from her mouth. She sat there on the velvet loveseat, transfixed, asphyxiated with delight. Finally, after a brief silence she managed to say, "Is it really true?"

Mrs. Bibi burst into laughter. "You know very well I'm not joking. Ezz confirmed it yesterday on the telephone. In a few weeks you'll be in Dubai."

Emma had a long list of questions, but she had the feeling that the moment was not right. She stood up and, not knowing exactly what she was doing, kissed Mrs. Bibi on the cheek.

Taken by surprise, the older woman didn't know quite how to respond. Then, without any great display of emotion, she responded in kind. "A thousand *mabruk*, Emma. I'm so happy for you."

Emma, overcome with a happiness that suffused every inch of her body, thanked Mrs. Bibi and her husband. Still laughing, Mrs. Bibi summoned her two daughters, who were quick to appear.

Stunned by the announcement, Emma followed the two girls into the adjacent room, which they used as a study. Her mind was far away and she hardly knew what she was saying. How she wished for the hours to fly by. She wanted only to hurry home and savour the wonderful news.

33

Emma couldn't keep her eyes off her watch. She could barely contain her impatience; the minute hand was moving too slowly. Soon the taxi that would take her and Sara to the airport would arrive. Two large suitcases stood poised in the vestibule. She had attempted to cram all she owned into those two cases—books, toys, clothing—everything folded and carefully packed. Her furniture was gone, all donated to the Salvation Army, returning whence it had come.

She would preserve her memories of Canada in her mind. It would be impossible to forget those years, from her first days in Montreal in a dormitory room to today, perched on a stool in a nearly empty house that would soon open its doors to another family, give shelter to other children, witness the unfolding of other lives. She would always remember the sleepless nights in the university computer centre as she put the finishing touches on her session projects. Nothing could remove from her memory the days following her marriage to Fadi: how happy she had been, how confident in the future, how proud of her life. She would never forget her joy at Sara's birth, nor the pain and the tears that followed her divorce. The conflicting feelings collided deep inside her; she couldn't drive them entirely away. Childhood memories tumbled over those of her life in Canada. She sat there staring out into space while Sara skipped rope in the kitchen.

Emma glanced out the window just as a glossy black car pulled up in front of the house. The taxi! The time had come. Emma stood up, double-checking her papers. Her passport, her daughter's passport, her work visa, everything was right where it should be. Sara stopped skipping and tucked the rope into a pocket of one of the suitcases.

"The taxi is waiting. Time to go," Emma exclaimed, as she adjusted her headscarf.

Slowly she opened the door and pushed the two suitcases onto the stoop. The driver, a husky man in his fifties with dark skin, got out of the car and came up to Emma. "*Salaam!* How are you, madam?"

"*Salaam.* I am fine, thank you," Emma replied. She was a bit startled to hear the driver greet her in the Islamic manner. It could only have been because of her headscarf that he recognized her as a Muslim, and he'd surely intended to put her at ease.

It was a beautiful day, the sun was shining, and the trees wore their full coat of green. Jeanne was smoking a cigarette as she watched her two daughters splashing in an inflatable pool on the front lawn. The driver carried Emma's suitcases to the car and placed them one after the other in the trunk. Emma waved to Jeanne, who walked over to say goodbye to her neighbour. Two worlds of sadness met as they fell into each other's arms.

"You'll send us a card from Dubai, promise?" said Jeanne with a motherly smile.

Sara was looking at her young neighbours as they bobbed in and out of the water, laughing and sputtering. A few leaves floated on the surface of the pool. Sara felt like staying to play with them.

"I will, for sure," stammered Emma, her throat constricted with emotion.

Jeanne broke into nervous laughter that finished with a spasm of coughing. Then, with a kind gaze, she watched Emma and Sara climb into the taxi. Jeanne and her daughters waved goodbye, and Emma and Sara followed suit. The driver took his seat and then the car drove off.

"Are you travelling, madam?" he asked.

"Yes," Emma answered in a low voice. "I'm going to work in Dubai."

She had hardly finished her sentence when the driver continued, "Oh, you're fortunate, madam! Me, I'm originally from Pakistan. Ali's my name and I'm trained as an engineer. When I came to Canada, I couldn't find work in my field, but, thank God, I'm earning my living now. As you can see, I'm an old man; I don't have any ambition. You've got to try your luck when you're young, your age..."

On and on he went, about his daughter, who was born in Ottawa and who had just received her degree in computer science and was getting married in a few months; about his wife, who was a wonderful cook. He ended every sentence with the same expression: "God be praised!"

Emma's mind was far away and she was barely listening. She held Sara's hand as she answered mechanically, "Yes. Yes, that's right." Her mind had already taken flight for Dubai. She could only think of the new life that was awaiting her over there. But then, suddenly, she felt unsure of her decision. Maybe she had acted too fast. But did she really have a choice? Caught between poverty and the humiliation of receiving welfare and a decent, well-paying job, what was she supposed to choose? She had been trapped, cornered. No doubt about it—the trip to Dubai was a life preserver.

Ali the driver pulled up in front of the international departures entrance, removed the two suitcases from the trunk, and placed them at Emma's feet. She already had the fare in hand.

"Thank you, madam, and most of all, good luck. Who knows, maybe you'll return to Ottawa one day. You never know..."

Emma smiled politely. She wanted to tell him that she was turning the page, that she would never turn back. But Ali and his taxi had already vanished.

She located a baggage cart and Sara helped her lift the two suitcases onto it. Pushed by four hands, the cart clunked slowly forward, carrying what remained of their life in Ottawa. The public address system blared through the airport. The countdown had begun.

Emma shivered and broke out in gooseflesh; suddenly she felt like dashing out of the airport. She thought of Jeanne, alone now with her two daughters, trapped in illness and poverty. Then she thought of her mother, how happy she was that her daughter would be closer to her and that she would be able to work in a dignified manner. Emma's hands clutched the handle of the luggage cart. She looked at Sara, smiled, and began to move at a decisive pace towards the check-in counter.

34

The festival season was in full swing. Tourists thronged Ottawa's ByWard Market. Some licked at ice-cream cones to cool off while others lounged beneath the umbrellas at sidewalk cafés as they watched the passing crowd.

The farmers' stalls overflowed with fresh produce from the surrounding countryside. The intense colours of the fruits and vegetables caught the eye of even the most indifferent passersby. Plump, sweet-smelling strawberries nudged up against tiny blueberries that glistened like dark pearls. Groups of tourists crowded around the stalls, popping samples into their mouths as they inquired about the price of this or that.

Then there were the florists' stands, with their flowering pots hanging like rainbows from the metal poles that held up the canopies that in turn protected their ephemeral existence. Elsewhere, flats of flowers were set out in ranks like well-disciplined soldiers as they waited patiently for someone to carry them away.

The window of a pastry shop exhibited its impeccably

decorated, almost joyous cakes, decorated with blanched hazelnuts and mango slices artfully laid atop chocolate curls. Lama and Louise were salivating as with their eyes they wolfed down the delicacies on display, wondering if they dared walk through the shop door and succumb to temptation.

"What do you think of that cake over there, the one with the fine layer of rose-coloured jelly?" asked Louise, turning to her friend.

Lama wrinkled her nose and hesitated. She would prefer one of the fat cigars stuffed with *crème pâtissière* and garnished at both ends with finely chopped almonds.

Since Louise had opened her heart to Lama about Ameur, the two girls saw each other almost every day. They would meet after class, chatting about everything and nothing, about their future, about politics, about boys, about religion. They agreed on most things, and about one thing in particular: they must never stop talking to each other.

Louise had begun a training course as a nurse in a palliative care unit. There she kept company with death on a daily basis and witnessed the suffering of the terminally ill. She did not regret her decision to become a nurse; in fact, every time she put on her work clothes and began looking after her patients, she felt her decision had been crucial. Still, metaphysical questions haunted her. Death was her constant companion. She witnessed it come to rest in sick bodies wracked by pain and reduced by suffering, even as the patients sought for hope in a word, a gesture, a glance. Louise sometimes found answers in her new faith, but just as often she did not, and it was then that she raised her doubts with Lama.

Her friend had found a job as a cashier in a small downtown

grocery store, where she worked from early morning until four o'clock in the afternoon. Her father had made up his mind to stay in Dubai for the summer and to take a winter vacation with the whole family over the New Year's holiday. Louise and Lama met every day at lunchtime to stroll along the Rideau Canal and enjoy a bite together. This day, they'd met at the ByWard Market and shared a tuna sandwich. Now it was time for dessert.

Finally, after much hemming and hawing, Lama opted for a mille-feuille with *crème pâtissière*, while Louise chose an almond tartlet. They stepped out of the pastry shop, as proud of their accomplished decision-making as if they had just completed an exhausting round of negotiations at the United Nations.

"Mmm, this *crème pâtissière* is delicious," said Lama, licking her lips. Louise was just finishing the last bite of her tartlet, and she nodded in agreement.

On Wellington they stopped not far from Parliament Hill. Hungry office workers were pouring out onto the streets. Two determined joggers strode past in the heat, their water bottles bouncing on their hips. As they ran by, red-faced and sweating, Louise exclaimed, "Wow, what determination! How I'd love to have the courage to deal with my problems and my convictions the way they do!"

"Why not? What's holding you back?" Lama responded as she shook pastry crumbs from her blouse.

"My mother's love . . . I just can't handle it by myself. Last fall I wanted to wear the veil. I made all the preparations, bought scarves, long skirts. I wanted to prove to myself who I was, to prove my new convictions, but I could never do it. Even my love for Ameur wasn't enough. I feel so weak, so unlike those runners defying the heat, the fatigue, and thirst."

"Why don't you explain your ideas to your mother? Why don't you try to talk it over with her, give her your side of the story?" asked Lama, forgetting for a moment that she could barely talk to her own mother.

"I did it, time and time again—tried to tell her. It's a big waste of time because she thinks I've been brainwashed...She doesn't want to accept that the path I've chosen isn't the same as hers. But in spite of everything I really love her, and I have the feeling that I can't really break free from her. It's like she's always looking at me critically, wherever I go and whatever I do—"

Lama opened her mouth and was about to speak when she noticed Louise's expression had changed. Her face was suddenly livid. They had just passed the Langevin Block, the building that houses the Privy Council and the Prime Minister's Office, and turned onto the Sparks Street pedestrian mall. Louise was staring at a man walking towards them. Lama recognized him—it was Ameur. He had on his customary blue pinstriped shirt and a pair of jeans; his hair was close-cropped. A smile on his face, he was heading straight for them.

35

It was a tiny shop, hardly noticeable from the outside and almost impossible to find, wedged in between a pizzeria and a video store. Passersby could easily mistake its entrance for the second door of one of the adjacent businesses. But once you had stepped through that narrow entrance, you were immediately transported a thousand leagues away from Ottawa, to faraway India or Pakistan.

The first thing to strike you would be a pungent odour that would follow you all the way home: the combined scent of cloves, cinnamon, curry powder, cumin seeds, and star anise, along with that of powdered mango, bay leaves, fresh papaya, and pudgy purple eggplant. It was a veritable Ali Baba's cavern of treasure, and its resident genie was the proprietor, a certain Mr. Kamal, a curious fellow with beady, darting eyes, a bald head, and a bulging belly that made him look like a down-and-out clown.

Fawzia Hussein was bustling up and down the narrow aisles, absorbed in her shopping. Her headscarf had slid onto her neck and shoulders. A few drops of sweat trickled down her broad, arching forehead, and she pulled a tissue from her purse and patted it dry. The fan Mr. Kamal had installed near the counter with the cash register was totally unequal to the task of dissipating the scorching heat that overwhelmed the city. Farther off, you could hear the humming of a venerable air conditioner, but its effect was intermittent at best, as if the merchandise that filled the shop to overflowing had intercepted the fresh air.

Mrs. Hussein paid no heed to the heat; after all, it reminded her of the land of her birth. She was feeling on top of the world. The things she had to buy were special—they were for the reception she was busy organizing for Sally's marriage to Sam. She could not afford to overlook a single ingredient! When she found a spice she was looking for or the particular kind of flour she needed to make a certain type of bread, in a low voice she summoned Ali Hussein, who, meek as a lamb, would break off his discussion with Mr. Kamal and come over to relieve his wife of her selection, then place it on the counter. A small pile of packages had already accumulated, but Fawzia kept on summoning her husband to pick up more purchases.

Now almost finished, she carried a large bag of basmati rice over to the counter and set it down alongside everything else. She had found all she needed. The next step would be to prepare the appetizers and store them in the freezer until the day of the reception.

Absorbed by the task, Mr. Kamal rang up her purchases with his sausage-like fingers as Ali placed them atop one another in plastic bags. The cab was parked outside; he had taken the morning off work to accompany his wife on her grocery-shopping expedition.

"Ali, did you put everything in the bags?" Fawzia asked.

Meanwhile Mr. Kamal was counting his money, his laughing eyes squinting so much that only a bit of skin and an eyelash or two showed.

"Yes, it's all there—the spices, the vegetables, the rice, the flour, everything," answered Ali, all smiles. When he stepped outside the shop, Fawzia was standing there, the bags at her feet. He opened the trunk and began to place them one beside the other. When he finished, he went back inside to say goodbye to Mr. Kamal.

The merchant was happy to have begun his day in such fine style. He was drinking water from a bottle, his head thrown back. When he heard Mr. Hussein step inside, he almost choked, pulled the bottle from his mouth, and wiped his lips.

"So sorry, my friend. I didn't mean to disturb you," Ali said, stretching out his hand. The two men bade each other a warm goodbye.

"Thanks so much. See you soon," called out Mrs. Hussein from just outside the store.

But Mr. Kamal didn't hear a word; he'd picked up the bottle of water and begun to drink again.

The couple got into the car. On the radio the announcer was saying, "And with the humidity, today's high will feel like about thirty-eight degrees."

Paying no attention, Fawzia Hussein mopped her brow again. "I'll begin with the sauces and prepare the rice and do the frying the day of the reception. I can heat everything else in the microwave. Is that okay?"

Ali handled the steering wheel expertly. "Everything you cook is terrific. It'll all be delicious, for sure." Fawzia accepted the compliment with as much delight as if she were hearing it for the first time.

The couple was overjoyed that their daughter had agreed to marry Sam. From the very first meeting, the two of them had agreed that Sam would be an ideal future husband for her. He was well brought-up, cultured, and polite, and best of all, he was a Muslim. Just recently, the university had awarded him a bursary to begin his master's program in computer science. He would be able to rent an apartment and marry Sally.

But Sally had been hesitant and wanted to think it over.

ON THE DAY of that first encounter, no sooner had Sam left than Fawzia and Ali sat down in the living room with their daughter. The trays with their few remaining slices of fresh fruit and the bowls of dried fruits and nuts were still on the coffee table. Ali scooped up a handful and began to nibble away like a mouse while Fawzia looked at her daughter in silence.

"So, what do you think of Sam?" Sally's father asked. "Do you like him?"

Sally had just lifted the veil from her head and face, and she blushed. Her father had taken her by surprise — she hadn't expected such a quick reaction. Her normally self-assured expression had evaporated and she seemed nonplussed. "I don't know. He seems nice enough, but no more..."

Fawzia, who'd been silent up to that point, piped up. "Take your time, sweetie, there's no hurry. We'll all have to think it over. After all, it's your future, not ours."

Ali slurped at the finger he'd stuck into his mouth to remove a piece of cashew lodged between two molars, then returned to nibbling on the salted nuts.

Fawzia picked up the trays and headed for the kitchen. "I'm going to do the dishes and clean up the house a bit."

Sally went off to her room, her parents' words spinning in her head. Things seemed to be moving too quickly. In fact, everything seemed to be whirling at top speed: her thoughts, the furniture, even the walls. She stretched out on her bed. All at once she regretted that she'd gone ahead and replied to The Boy Next Door. Then she spied her BlackBerry on the night table. Things were getting serious. Marriage was looming on the horizon. She felt a powerful urge to muster all her remaining energy and smash that little machine. She restrained herself but didn't even want to look at it. She tossed it into her night table, alongside the collection of miniature elephants. It was pure impulse, but it brought her a bit of relief.

Then she heard the BlackBerry hum. It was the alert for a new message. She hesitated. What should she do now? Ignore it or read it? Her heart began to beat faster. A few seconds later she pulled open the drawer, took the BlackBerry between her hands, opened the inbox, and read the sender's address.

The anonymous messages were over. Everything was clear: the email was from Sam Lamarche.

36

"What are you trying to say, anyway? Emma would never do such a thing! She's so well-behaved, so discreet. Why, you hardly notice she's there. Plus she's not really what you'd call a great beauty... Eh? Just what are you hinting at? No, really! Listen, I know my husband. He adores me, even though we're far apart. He'd never even look at another woman... Do me a favour, will you? Let's change the subject. By the way, what's Suzie's new friend's name? The one from Montreal, I mean."

Samia Bibi was lounging in her backyard in the shade of a broad parasol. No one could see her, so she was not wearing her headscarf. Her glossy hair fell across her forehead. Her clear, bright voice rose and fell among the flowerbeds, the sculpted bushes, and the arching trees that protected the garden from the eyes of passersby. She was wearing Bermuda shorts; her pale legs that only rarely saw the sun rested upon a low wicker table that also held a tall glass of water, a small vial of nail polish, a pack of cigarettes, and an ashtray. Seated on a rattan sofa upholstered with plump cushions covered with maroon fabric, cellphone glued to her left ear and a cigarette in her right hand, she'd been chatting for a good twenty minutes with her friend Leila.

Leila was familiar with Emma's story. She knew Samia had helped her find work in Dubai with her husband's company. It was a friendly warning, no more—Emma might just steal her husband. After all, she knew almost nothing of "this divorcee's" past. Samia Bibi was upset by Leila's thinly veiled insinuations. What business was it of hers, sticking her nose into matters that didn't concern her? *I never asked her for her opinion, so why is she always hinting that maybe Emma will try to take Ezz away from me? How can she judge Emma, or my husband? She doesn't even know them!*

She put down the telephone. She was getting angrier and angrier with Leila. With a sudden gesture that revealed her frayed nerves, she pushed her hair behind her ears, then lit another cigarette as she thought over what Leila had said. *Are you crazy or what, helping a divorced woman get work in your husband's company? You don't know what Tunisians are like. They're headstrong women, emancipated. I hear that some of them even use black magic to steal the hearts of the men they want . . .* the words stung like darts. Of course she knew Leila was blowing things out of proportion; it was nothing but stories she'd heard from people who couldn't be trusted in the first place. Gossip. Nothing but gossip.

Emma was a respectable woman, and she knew it. She could see it in her eyes at their very first meeting: an educated woman who'd run into bad luck, a girl from a good family who had no bad intentions. *Just who does Leila think she is, anyway? That prim and prissy one who divorces her first husband on account of impotence, then goes and marries his brother!* But for all the arguments that Samia could muster, Leila's words sent chills down her spine. *Ezz has never cheated on me. He loves me and he loves the girls. All he wants is our happiness. Okay, so we only see each other during vacations, and I don't know for sure what he does there all alone in Dubai. One thing's certain though: he works day and night to make us happy.*

The thought made tears well up in Samia's eyes. It was as if, for the first time in years, she realized the absurdity of their life and the distance that separated her from her husband. She wanted to call him, to hear his voice, to seek shelter from Leila's insidious remarks, which reminded her of the hissing of a snake. The unexpected surge of emotion had nudged aside the superficiality of Samia's daily life.

She was just about to dial her husband's number when the voices of her daughters coming towards her made her change her mind. She stopped cold.

"Oh, Mommy, you're all pink! What is it?" asked Mona.

"It's nothing. I think I've been in the sun too long. I should have put on some sunscreen; the parasol's not enough," Samia answered, butting out her cigarette in the ashtray. It was a purely mechanical gesture, but it relieved the tension.

To change the subject, Samia bombarded her daughters with questions. "Did you like the film? What about your friends, did they show up? Are you going to see them again next week? Did you have a bite to eat after the movie?"

Lynne and Mona didn't have time to answer. Samia glanced at her watch and saw that it was nearly six o'clock. Lama hadn't come back from work yet. "I wonder what she's up to?"

She stood up and gathered her hair, fastening it with the

grip she'd stuck between the cushions of the sofa, and slipped on a pair of turquoise sandals. The woven leather straps enveloped her dainty feet and the colour brought out her fuchsia nail polish. Without a word she headed for the house as Lynne and Mona looked on, blank expressions on their faces. Then they burst out laughing.

"She's acting really weird. What's going on?" Lynne asked Mona, frowning.

Her sister rolled her eyes. "I don't have the faintest idea. But you know something? I don't want to know! Angelina Jolie was great in the movie, wasn't she?" And Mona launched into a dialogue with her sister that was punctuated by exclamations and cries of admiration.

Samia was happy to be back in the cool of her kitchen. She wanted to forget Leila and her stupid remarks. She opened the fridge. The carafe of syrup she'd prepared the previous day from apricot leather hadn't been touched. She picked it up, plopped two ice cubes into a glass, and filled it with the satin-smooth, unctuous orange liquid. She took one mouthful, then a second. With a click of her tongue she indicated her satisfaction, then, like a cat recovering from a sudden leap, she went upstairs to her room to take a shower.

37

From the window Emma looked down at the lights of Dubai scintillating in the darkness. It was after midnight and the airplane would be landing in a few minutes. The spectacle below dazzled her: thousands of bright lights shining against the darkness of the heavens, as if the eyes of an infinite number of nocturnal creatures were peering curiously up at the sky. The soaring skyscrapers, each one extravagantly taller than the next, seemed to rub up against the firmament. Her mouth half-open in wonderment, Emma was like a country girl seeing the city for the first time.

Sara was fast asleep beside her, head tilted slightly back against the seat, resting on her hands. The trip had been without incident; everything had gone smoothly. For one last time Emma threw a furtive glance at the marvellous spectacle that was unfolding on the other side of the window.

Inside the plane, the passengers were quiet. The sound of snoring came from a few rows back, probably from a tired passenger who was sleeping right until the last minute. The clear voice of the flight attendant broke the nearly embarrassing silence that had fallen over the cabin. "Ladies and gentlemen, on behalf of the crew, I welcome you to Dubai International Airport," and then she continued in Arabic, *"Ahlan wa sahlan bikum!"*

Emma's heart missed a beat. The words of welcome reminded her that she had truly left Canada and soon she would be setting foot in another country. What could fate possibly have in store for her?

"Sara, Sara, my darling, wake up! We're here."

In confusion Sara opened her eyes. She'd lost track of time and no longer knew whether it was day or night. But soon she was wide awake, with a broad smile on her lips. "Mummy, are we in Dubai? Did you see the tower, the one we saw on the computer?" she asked with her innocent look.

Emma couldn't suppress a smile. The sight of Sara buoyed her hopes, and she felt the tension easing. She would have to be strong. "It's night outside, sweetie. I couldn't make out the tower, but I saw plenty of tall buildings. It's really impressive, you'll see."

Sara was enchanted. She'd forgotten her fatigue and her eyes were round with curiosity. All the passengers were on their feet now. Emma opened her purse to check her travel documents. She was terrified of losing even one. Her entire life—the past, the present, and the future—hung on those pieces of paper. She sighed, reassured; everything was exactly as she'd left it.

The line of passengers moved forward slowly. The crying of a baby, awakened by the hustle and bustle or calling for its bottle, added to the commotion as they made their way out of the aircraft. Emma could hear several languages being spoken, the main ones being Arabic and English. Her ear, confused, picked up snatches of conversation in Arabic mixed with English. *I'll get used to it,* she reassured herself. The door of the aircraft wasn't too far away.

Emma took Sara's hand and they soon found themselves walking down a corridor. Emma followed the signs leading to Customs and Immigration. The interminable passageway finally opened onto an immense arrival hall, in the middle of which stood a huge silver artificial palm tree surrounded by shops displaying the most prestigious brand names. Atop a pedestal was a silver-grey sports car that caught the passengers' eyes as it proclaimed its insolent beauty, seeming to say, *Come to me, take me. I am yours. This is Dubai, the land of marvels, the place where everything is possible."*

Emma and Sara squeezed each other's hands harder still. "Mummy, it's like a great big carousel!"

Emma nodded as she tried to locate the direction to Customs. The luxury on display all around her made her ill at ease. The sign pointing in the right direction appeared amid bright ceiling lights that reflected off the polished white marble floor.

A woman walked by nonchalantly, wearing a long black dress that covered her from head to toe, leaving only her eyes showing. The little girl beside her was clutching the woman's dress with one hand while she held a Barbie doll in the other. The woman looked in all directions as if she was expecting someone. A man came up to her with a smile on his face and Emma heard him speak to the woman in Arabic. "Our flight is on time. I just checked with an agent."

Emma felt a twinge of discomfort. The sight of a woman with a man reminded her that she was alone with her daughter in this strange city. There was no man to guide her, so she would have to be her own guide. She picked up the pace. Both she and Sara needed to rest.

"Mummy, when do we get outside? I'm thirsty."

Emma's face paled as they approached Customs. "Just be patient a little bit longer. We'll be at our hotel soon."

Now they were standing in front of the wicket. The customs official, a man with a thick moustache and a white scarf covering his hair, motioned her to come forward. Emma could feel her stomach churning. With his dark eyes he looked her over. Emma's hands were shaking.

"Your passports, please," he said, with the thick Arab accent peculiar to the countries of the Gulf.

Emma handed him her and Sara's blue Canadian passports. When he noticed Emma's nationality, his manner became more relaxed. He seemed accommodating, almost courteous. "Do you have your husband's written permission for your daughter?" he asked, pointing at Sara, a forced smile revealing blackened teeth.

Emma handed him the document. She didn't want to mention that the man was no longer her husband. "Above all, don't tell anyone you're divorced. Keep it quiet," Samia Bibi had whispered in her ear during their final meeting in Ottawa.

The man in the glass booth seemed satisfied. He stroked his moustache and handed Emma's documents back to her. This time his gaze was one of curiosity, even a bit prying. Then, with a flick of the wrist, he waved her through.

Her two suitcases were waiting patiently on the revolving

carousel. She lifted them onto a baggage cart and headed for the exit. Sara, who had watched the whole scene without a peep, felt relieved. She looked up at her mother timidly. "And now are we going to our hotel?"

Emma was pleased to have passed this first exam successfully. "Yes, we are, sweetie. We'll be there in a few minutes."

The two passed through the automatic sliding doors, out of the airport and into the hot, dry air outside. Even though it was nighttime, the temperature was high. Palm trees planted at regular intervals dotted the landscape. A faint whiff of dust filtered into Emma's nose, as if to remind her that they were in the heart of the desert; she coughed softly.

A taxi pulled up. The driver looked like Ali, the talkative cabbie who had driven them to the Ottawa airport. He smiled and placed the two suitcases in the trunk of his car. "Where to, madam?" he asked.

Emma had trouble understanding him. Finally she figured out what he was saying. "Ramada Inn, please. Al-Mankhool Street."

The driver did not say a word and, with a bored look on his face, drove off. What a contrast with Ali, who hadn't stopped talking for the entire trip to the airport. Here people kept to themselves, she concluded. Better not trust anyone. *So much the better. He won't ask any questions,* Emma mused philosophically.

It was all Sara could do to keep her eyes open. Emma leaned back against the seat of the taxi. A smile crept over her mouth. The adventure was about to begin.

38

Ameur's brilliant smile revealed his white, straight teeth. He looked for all the world like a well-trained dog that had just rediscovered his master. His charmer's gaze came to rest on Louise while Lama stood motionless, like a pillar of salt. Louise, in her confusion, had no idea what to do. She wanted to appear indifferent, but her face betrayed a mixture of love, rekindled by this sudden apparition, and contempt for Ameur's feckless nature.

"What a wonderful surprise! How are you doing?" Ameur's melodious voice revealed nothing of what had gone before.

Louise stammered, looking for words, forcing a smile. She hoped Lama would come to the rescue, but her friend was watching the passing crowd. "I'm okay, thank you. And you?" she managed to articulate after a few seconds.

"We don't see you at meetings any more. How come?"

Lama, who was listening while feigning inattention, was seething with anger. She wanted to ask him, *Will your mother allow Louise to go to meetings?* but she bit her tongue.

"I've been really busy with my lectures, and now my training course is taking up all my time. The others will have to take up the slack."

Ameur knew very well that she hadn't wanted to see him again after the breakup. He carried on as if everything was perfectly normal. "You're always welcome. Your presence and your contribution are important for the association. Isn't that so, Lama?" he said, looking at Louise's friend.

Lama chewed on her lip and said nothing. She didn't want to hurt Ameur in front of Louise, as she suspected her friend still loved him, but she detested his hypocrisy and wanted nothing better than to end the conversation then and there.

All at once Ameur's voice turned serious, his forehead wrinkled. Turning to Louise, he said, "We absolutely have to meet before I leave for Hamilton. Call me on my cell. I've got to run now; I've got a meeting in a couple of minutes." He said goodbye and rushed off.

Louise hardly knew what to make of his parting words. "Hamilton? Do you think he's been accepted to med school?"

Louise and Lama resumed their stroll, but the relaxed and cheerful atmosphere had dissipated. The two girls paid no attention to the passersby, or to the Sparks Street boutiques that were displaying their merchandise on the sidewalk. The encounter with Ameur had spoiled everything.

"He's a brainy guy. Why wouldn't he enrol in med school down there? Louise, are you really going to call him?" Lama was upset. Louise hadn't forgotten Ameur, that melting smile of his, that syrupy voice. She'd just witnessed it with her own eyes.

"I don't know if I'll be able to talk to him. I don't even know what I'd say," ventured Louise. "What do you think, Lama?"

Louise's question bore down more heavily on Lama than the heat of the day. She did not respond immediately. Instead she watched the watercraft gliding by on the silvery surface of the Rideau Canal. On both banks bicycles rushed by, as if to prove how much faster they were than the tourist-filled boats.

"Frankly, I don't know. You have to make your mind up, Louise. I've never had anyone to love, so I'm not the right person to give you an answer."

Louise blushed. In the confusion and the heat, the word, the gesture from Lama she'd hoped for was slow in coming. She'd never imagined that a chance meeting with Ameur could have such an impact. Now she was caught in the claws of her own feelings. Her love for Ameur was alive—she'd just experienced the proof.

The bus was coming, so she rummaged through her purse for her pass. "I'll be phoning," she called out as she boarded the bus.

Lama stood there, feet pinned to the ground. She threw a last glance at the Rideau Canal; it shone in the midday sun like a silvery knife slicing through the city. *That water makes me want to dive in,* she thought. She checked her watch and hurried off. The lunch hour was almost over.

39

Emma buttoned her tailored beige jacket. She had a meeting at the office in one hour, and she did not want to be late. She smiled at herself in the mirror. Her appearance — simple but professional — pleased her. Two months had passed since she'd arrived in Dubai, and things could not have been better. She enjoyed her work and Mr. Bibi treated her well. He'd briefed her on her job, on relations with her co-workers, promotions — in a word, on everything she needed to know to play an effective role in the company.

Her salary was excellent. She'd located a small furnished apartment not far from the office, bought a small car, and enrolled Sara in a day camp where she could swim, play tennis, and even ice skate. Early every morning Emma left the apartment, drove her daughter to camp, and then headed for the office. In the afternoon she finished work at around four o'clock, picked up Sara, and the two of them returned home, tired but happy to be together.

As a rule Emma would go out with Sara in the evening for

a shopping trip or for a stroll in one of the city's malls. Both of them loved their new life. It felt as if they were on holiday, where every day brought a new discovery. There was only one drawback—the weather. No sooner did they step outdoors to get into the car than a wave of dry, burning heat would sweep over them, leaving them gasping for breath, enveloping their bodies as if they were dead trees on a sunscorched field. Fortunately the punishment lasted only a few minutes, and then everything returned to normal. The airconditioned buildings welcomed them with open arms, cooling them and helping them forget that only a few moments earlier they had tasted the flames of Hell.

Emma chatted with her mother regularly, and at length.

"Mum, you've got to come and visit me here in Dubai. No more excuses. It's nothing like the Canadian cold!"

Her mother felt much better now that Emma had found a well-paying job that matched her skills. "Better if you come to Tunis. I really miss you. How much I'd love to hug you, to touch you," said the older woman, who'd never flown in her life and was not intending to do so now, now that she was well into her sixties.

"God willing, when I can put some money aside and my boss gives me a vacation, that's the first thing I'll do," Emma murmured, dreaming of that day.

She gave herself one last glance in the mirror, smoothed her skirt to remove an unwelcome crease, slung her purse over her shoulder, and closed the door. Sara had already left for camp while Emma stayed home with Mr. Bibi's permission to prepare for an important meeting.

It was a meeting with representatives of a Canadian software company that hoped to sign a contract with the al-Arish Group. Mr. Bibi had asked Emma to study the project and insisted that she attend. Her Canadian experience would make it easier for her to evaluate the company. Emma was determined to do her best. She did not want to miss the chance to demonstrate her qualifications and her abilities to Mr. Bibi, his associate, and their colleagues.

The highway that led to the office was a little less congested by then. Her car, a midget among giants, wound its way between four-wheel-drive vehicles with tinted glass windows that looked more like tanks. More than once she narrowly avoided being crushed by a monster car bearing down on her at full speed. The streets, the interchanges, and the overpasses met, converged, and branched off in all directions. Sixteen-lane motorways sliced through heavily built-up areas where skyscrapers marched off into the distance.

Emma was relieved to find space in the company parking lot. She parked her car and almost ran towards the entrance. The marble floor glowed and the glass doors gleamed in the sunlight. The Indian receptionist greeted her with a polite hello. Emma took the elevator to the sixteenth floor. "Come see me before the meeting. We'll go together," Mr. Bibi had said to her the previous day as she was about to leave. Now she headed straight for her boss's office.

Emma knocked on the door and went in. She stood there like a well-behaved schoolgirl waiting for instructions from her superior. He looked up to acknowledge her presence, then said, "I just have to finish an important message, then I'll be ready. You can take a seat."

She sat down and waited. Mr. Bibi was seated in front of

his computer screen. His round glasses with the wire frames lent him a bookish appearance. He was wearing a conservative grey suit, his well-cut hair was combed back, and he had a contented look on his face. Next to his computer stood a family portrait. The office exuded luxury. The mahogany floor matched his desk and bookshelves. A photo showing two men in traditional Emirati dress, heads covered with *agals*, hung from the wall. The two men were smiling and shaking hands. It was Mr. al-Arish, the CEO, greeting the prince of Dubai.

Green plants in all the corners embellished the artificial atmosphere of the room. Tiny recessed halogen lights shone like distant stars from the ceiling, bathing the office in subdued light. White venetian blinds hung across the tinted windows to block the intensity of the sun's rays as they broke like waves against the glass, attempting to penetrate the building.

Emma remained seated, lost in thought. Only a few months ago she had been penniless and depressed. Like a shipwreck survivor she had struggled to make ends meet, thanks to her monthly social welfare payments and the few dollars she earned tutoring. But now she lived in Dubai, this marvellous city, and like Alice in Wonderland, she had begun to find her way through the trackless desert. Hope flowed in her veins and life seemed bright once more.

"The Canadians are waiting for us." Mr. Bibi had drawn himself up to his full height in front of her. He seemed a bit tense. Emma shook herself from her reverie and followed him towards the meeting room with its massive oval table, its conference phones, and its high-backed executive chairs.

When Mr. Bibi and Emma entered the room, the members

of the delegation were already seated, each with his laptop open in front of him. Ahmed and Lili, two of Emma's colleagues, were already there.

Emma took a deep breath. She was determined to do her best and to succeed.

40

What kind of ceremony would you like? Sally typed, her slender fingers moving rapidly and unerringly across the keyboard. She'd been chatting with Sam, her future husband, for the past few minutes. Sally was much more comfortable with him when they exchanged messages on the computer. She was no longer apprehensive, embarrassed, or timid, as she had been when Sam first sent his anonymous messages. Her stomach wasn't in turmoil, her head didn't spin, nor did her hands sweat or her heart beat faster the way they had when she read the first poems from The Boy Next Door.

For an entire week following Sam's visit to her parents, Sally had not answered his messages. Everything had happened so fast, and she was frightened. And then one night she had a curious dream: She saw herself all alone, dancing in the centre of an immense room. A knock came at the door. "Who is it?" she asked. No answer. Then suddenly Sam's face appeared, as though in supplication. She awoke late in the night, happy and at peace. She was convinced the dream was a premonition, and she promised herself she would relate it to one of the sheikhs she corresponded with on the Web.

The sheikh's answer could not have been clearer: *My daughter, he is the one for you. He has asked for your hand, do not let him go, and by the grace of God everything will be fine.*

Tears came to Sally's eyes. She had only described her dream. The online sheikh knew nothing about Sam but was explicitly advising her to marry him. It was then that she answered Sam's messages. She was by turns open, considerate, and effervescent, finally emerging from the hard and brittle shell she had formed after his visit. Ever since then her parents, Fawzia and Ali, had been preparing the house to receive the wedding guests. Only a few weeks remained.

We could have two small ceremonies, one in the afternoon for the men and the other in the evening for the women, wrote Sam in response to Sally's question.

She smiled, delighted. Sam respected her views and did everything she wished, offering suggestions that perfectly matched her vision of the world. *I couldn't agree more,* she answered immediately.

But before Sally could type another question, Sam surprised her with a poem. *My dream, my hope, my moon in the sky...*

Sally felt as though she'd been swept up into a world of wonder. Sam had a gift—the gift of making her dream.

She was just finishing a message when she heard her name. Her mother was calling her from the front door. She sent off a few quick words to Sam to tell him she had to go, then hurried down the stairs with their storm-grey carpeting.

Her mother was holding two shopping bags, her father

several more. In a few moments the hall was filled with shopping bags, overflowing with ingredients and condiments of every size, shape, and description.

"Sally, can you take these bags to the kitchen?" Fawzia looked dazed and frazzled as she stood in the midst of the wave of white plastic.

Her husband carried in the rest of the bags and started to laugh. "Well, what are you waiting for? Is it the heat that's stopped you in your tracks?" He continued to laugh but Fawzia made no reply, so he handed the bags to Sally. She carried them into the kitchen, then came back for more.

Ali picked his way carefully through the heaps of groceries. "I'm going to take a shower and rest a while. I'll go to work a bit later." His mission accomplished, he made his way up the stairs, waddling like an old monkey.

Sally and Fawzia were alone in the kitchen. Fawzia was stretching her legs to relieve the stress she felt in her entire body. As she massaged her swollen knees with arthritis-gnarled hands, she gave Sally instructions. "Open the cinnamon jar in the pantry and fill it with the sticks I just bought—they're so fresh the smell makes my nose itch! Then take the big jug of oil and put it in the basement. I'll need it later."

Sally did exactly as she was told, and as she did she rediscovered the docility of her childhood. Sam's love had erased all traces of arrogance, swept away resentment.

"Mommy, what do you think of two small ceremonies instead of one mixed? One for the men, the other for the women."

Fawzia stopped rubbing her knees and stared at her daughter with laughter in her eyes. "I've never heard of such a thing.

Two ceremonies on the same day!" Then she shrugged her shoulders and declared, "It doesn't matter. I'd do anything to make you happy."

Sally took her mother in her arms and kissed her forehead tenderly. Fawzia broke out in goosebumps—her daughter hadn't hugged her for months. She forgot her swollen knees, stood up, and helped Sally put the groceries away.

41

Daddy dearest,

I'm really upset that you put off your holidays until December. I haven't seen you for a year now and I really miss you. But because I love you I forgive you and I'll pardon you, on condition that you keep your promise this time. Lucky for me I've got my job at the store—I'm busy all day long and when I come home at night I'm so tired all I can think about is sleeping.

There's something else that keeps my mind off your absence: my new friend Louise. We meet a lot at midday for lunch and take long walks in the downtown area before we go back to work. We get along fine, and Louise has become my best friend. She's completed all her courses and now all she has to do is complete her internship program, then she can start work as a nurse. I'm really happy for her because that was always her dream—to help other people and to ease their pain.

The fall session is almost here. In a few weeks I'll be diving into my books and my study notes. This will be a year of decision for Lynne. She'll have to work really hard if she wants to get admitted to the program she wants. I talked to her about it and she agrees. We'll see, but I don't know what she'll do without Emma. By the way, how is she doing? Has she adapted? I really hope so, for her sake.

The other day on the phone you sounded so tired, and you mentioned you had a meeting with a delegation from Canada. Funny, isn't it, those Canadians going all the way to Dubai to sign a contract with your company and here in Canada you couldn't even find work!

My summer job ends ten days before classes start up. Mommy promised to take us to Montreal for two days. Well, that's one way of having a holiday together, but I don't really know if I'm interested in spending all my spare time strolling through shopping centres. I'll have more to say, for sure. Please call! Even if you're really busy.

Your daughter,

Lama

"What are you doing?" Samia asked her daughter, who was writing the final words of her letter.

Lama, pretending not to hear, slipped her pen back into the pencil case and put the letter pad into the large red bag she used both as a handbag and for carrying her books during the school year. She was sitting on one of the living room sofas, about to get up for some breakfast before she went off to work.

Samia appeared upset that her daughter did not answer her. In a higher than normal voice with a shrill edge of exasperation, she said, "You're not answering your mother, or what?"

Lama feigned surprise. "You were talking to me? I didn't hear." Lama had learned how to avoid confrontation. She would slip out adroitly in order to avoid the futile quarrels and the interminable exchanges that would always end with one of Samia's monologues lamenting about life, fate, and disrespectful youngsters who had no consideration for their parents.

"I'm going to get a bite, then I'm off to work."

Samia admonished her. "Don't come in late like last time. It's not proper for a young lady of your age."

But Lama was already in the kitchen, where she spread yogurt on a piece of pita and dusted it with a few pinches of dried thyme. Then she rolled it up and took a bite out of the fat cigar. "I told you, there was a fight on the bus last time. That's why I was late." Her mouth was full as she spoke. She poured some tea into a saucer and swallowed it to get the lump of bread down, then added, "No, don't worry. Everything will be fine."

Lama's last words were lost on Samia. Her mother had already returned to her room, telephone in hand, not knowing quite what to do. *If I call him to see how he's doing, he'll get suspicious. Maybe he'll think there's some problem at home.* She stopped short and placed the handset atop her dresser. *That Leila, always putting nasty ideas in my mind. I've got to be smarter than her. I know Ezz too well—he would never do such a thing.* But Samia couldn't get Leila's perfidious words out of her head.

She stood in front of a rack of dresses in her walk-in closet. Packed in against one another were gowns of every colour and description, something for every occasion. She selected a long green dress and then, like an automaton, picked up the telephone. She'd made up her mind: she was going to speak to her husband. After all, what could be more normal than for a wife to wonder what her husband was up to? She glanced at her watch; it was nine o'clock in Ottawa, which meant that it was five o'clock in the afternoon Dubai time. She dialled the number. There was a faint click, then a long ring followed by silence, then another ring.

Where could he be at this time of day? Usually he's the last one to leave the office. She held the handset to her ear for several seconds. The sound of ringing, over and over again, worried her.

She didn't feel like going over to her friend Suzie's for coffee. She put the long green dress back in the closet. *I'll call her, tell her I'm not feeling well . . .* She pulled a pack of cigarettes out of her handbag.

Her fingers were shaking. She opened the balcony door, lit up, inhaled deeply, and ran her hand across her forehead. The pulse in her temples was throbbing like a tambourine. "I never should have helped Emma go to Dubai. I should have gone myself, with the girls," she murmured, hunched over, one hand on the balustrade and her cigarette in the other.

42

Alice Gendron had understood for some time that her daughter was no longer seeing Ameur. She was relieved. It was only a matter of time before Louise gave up this new religion of hers and their relationship could get back to normal. Besides, the two women were more and more on the same wavelength. They chatted a bit in the morning before leaving for work, and at night they would eat together most of the time.

A few nights ago Alice had even shared a humorous recollection with her daughter. She had almost missed her bus when her jacket caught on a piece of metal protruding from the bus shelter. "I thought someone was holding me back, and I was thrashing around for dear life. People were staring at me — I must have looked completely crazy."

Alice convulsed with laughter as Louise, half surprised and half curious, listened to her mother, fascinated. "So how did you finally get loose?"

"Lucky for me, a man standing nearby figured out what was happening and unhooked my jacket. It was too much, let me tell you!" Alice finally managed to explain between bursts of laughter.

Louise laughed along with her, delighted to see her mother happy in her company.

"The bus driver waited for me. I was really a sight!" Alice shook her head and wiped a tear of mirth from her eye.

But happy interludes like that one didn't last long. All Louise had to do was retire to her room to pray or be discovered reading the Qur'an in the living room for coldness to fall between the two. They would avoid each other's eyes, Alice's nostrils would flare, both their bodies would stiffen, and mother and daughter would become strangers once again, unable to speak to one another across the chasm gaping open between them.

Alice had come home from work early so she could take the rest of the day off. She felt like making the most of one of the last fine days of summer. She'd returned home, taken a shower, and, feeling fresher, picked up a book and sat down on the balcony.

Her balcony garden was a miniature work of art. It did everything a garden should: it was cool and calming and had an ambiance that was propitious for daydreaming. Flowers, herbs, and green plants thrived in clay pots. There was even a container of cherry tomatoes; the tiny red globes dancing in the breeze could have been rubies, half hidden amongst foliage suspended between the concrete walls of the city. Sitting on the balcony and reading went hand in hand. She forgot time and worry, escaping for hours on end only to emerge rested, relaxed, at peace and on the verge of sleep.

A few ice cubes floated in a tall glass of water. Alice hadn't noticed the time go by — the novel she was reading had carried her off into another world. Suddenly she heard Louise's footsteps in the hallway.

"Mum, are you there?"

Alice glanced at her watch. Five o'clock. Louise was coming home from work. Without moving, she replied, "I'm here, on the balcony."

Louise joined her mother. The two women looked each other over. Alice quickly grasped that Louise wasn't her usual self. She looked drawn. There was something on her mind. "How was your day?" she asked.

Not wanting to mention the meeting with Ameur, her daughter found a good alibi. "It's terrible what I see every day. There's so much suffering. One of my patients died. It was more than he could bear—" She stopped short and tears filled her eyes. How she would have liked to share her emotions with her mother, talk to her about meeting Ameur, about her feelings towards him, about the question he'd asked her before leaving…but her mother would lose her temper and their relationship would suffer yet again. Talking about work was less risky, a path with fewer pitfalls. Her mother would understand and give her advice.

"But, darling, that's life. You do everything you can, but there comes a time when you can do no more…"

Tears were now running down Louise's cheeks. She wiped them with the back of her hand. "You're right, Mummy, I take everything too personally. I think I'll go and lie down for a while."

It was an excellent excuse for her to be alone. The afternoon's encounter had thrown Louise's plans into turmoil.

Ameur's face, his smile, his voice, his eyes—everything about him still drew her in. And she had thought she was immunized! Love still lurked within her, concealed in a writhing nest of emotions, but like a tamed tiger, it crouched, ready to pounce at the first sight of a chunk of raw meat.

Should I see him again or just turn the page? she wondered as she lay on her bed. *Why would he try to talk to me if everything is over between us?* Then a new thought flashed through her mind. *What if he has something important to tell me?*

Again and again she went over the encounter with a fine-toothed comb, analyzing every word, visualizing all the possible outcomes, imagining herself once again with Ameur, married and happy. Then she remembered the expression on Lama's face. She hadn't seemed too enthusiastic about her talking with Ameur. *I should listen to Lama. She's the one who stuck by me when he betrayed me,* she concluded.

Alice's voice shook her out of her daydream. She got up and looked in the mirror. She felt lost.

Her mother's voice rang out again. "Louise, have you seen the TV remote?"

Shaking herself out of her stupor, Louise hurried out to the living room.

43

"You were simply mag-ni-fi-cent! We really clinched the deal!"
Mr. Bibi gazed at Emma in admiration. A new kind of spark
glistened in his black eyes. Emma couldn't recall ever having
seen him in such a state since she'd begun to work for him.

No one had ever complimented her so generously on her
work, not even Fadi, her ex-husband. She had finally adjusted,
but in reality she liked to be encouraged with a smile or a
word of congratulation, the way her father in Tunisia had
reacted when she came home from school with good marks.
He would pat her on the head, pay her extra attention, and
pray for her. Alas, her father was gone, and Emma no longer
heard those words of praise that had touched her heart and
urged her forward.

Fadi and her former employer had both been parsimonious
with their compliments, and at first Emma had believed that
Mr. Bibi was like them. He was courteous and considerate
towards her, of course. He explained her job, taking time to
discuss the smallest details, but he addressed her as he did all

his other employees, with a hint of indifference in his voice. But the meeting that had just ended was revealing another facet of Mr. Bibi.

The Canadian delegation had left for their hotel and the other employees had returned to their desks. Emma found herself alone with her boss. He made a point of telling her how much he appreciated her contribution and the points she had raised during the meeting.

Emma blushed, stammering, "Thank you, Mr. Bibi, I'm flattered. I've done a lot of reading about this technology, so I know its strengths and weaknesses quite well."

She was anxious to leave—Sara was waiting—but Mr. Bibi was prolonging the discussion. He was visibly pleased, as though he had just discovered that Emma existed. He wanted to talk to her, as though he needed someone to listen. "From now on you'll be attending all our meetings and teleconferences with our Canadian partners. I really need your expertise." He looked at her again with admiring eyes, bid her goodbye, and left the room, leaving her standing there stunned.

The deluge of compliments had overwhelmed Emma. She remained motionless for a moment, Mr. Bibi's words ringing in her ears. Then the thought of Sara brought her back to reality.

Sara was upset because she was the last to leave the day camp. The monitor, a young Lebanese with slicked-back hair and a patronizing attitude, scolded Emma in an arrogant tone: "Madam, the camp closes at five o'clock. A few minutes' delay is tolerated, but not more."

Emma could hardly be bothered to look at him. She hugged her daughter, took her by the hand, and hurried off.

"I'm sorry, sweetie, but I had an important meeting. We were busy all day. Next time I'll be here on the dot."

Sara quickly forgot the incident and began to describe her day, the camp activities and games. Emma listened distractedly. She could not forget the way Mr. Bibi had looked at her. Why his sudden change in attitude? What could she not forget that strange glitter in her boss's eyes?

Emma was relieved to be home with Sara at last. She closed the apartment door behind her and stretched out on the khaki-coloured velvet sofa. The apartment was small and simply furnished, but it was all Emma and her daughter needed: two small bedrooms and a living room with an adjoining open kitchen. She had purchased only the barest essentials, which included a large bed, a small bed, two night tables, a bookcase, and several sets of shelves.

Emma had also bought a laptop, which she kept on the kitchen table. When she and Sara ate, she moved it to the counter, and then, once the meal was over and the table cleared, moved it back. At night when Sara was sleeping, Emma would spend two hours on the Web, reading up on the latest technological developments in her field in an effort to make up for time lost during the past two tumultuous years. Her self-confidence returned.

In addition to the furniture, Emma had bought pots and pans, china, utensils, and even a few small electrical appliances — all of it cheap — in the malls where she did her shopping. She had a well-equipped kitchen in which she could prepare tasty dishes for herself and her daughter.

Emma did not feel like cooking tonight. The events of the day, which should have brought her pleasure and made her happy, had perturbed her and left her feeling awkward and uncomfortable.

"Mummy, make me rice with chicken and mushroom sauce. We haven't eaten that for a long time!" Sara put on a pouty face that made her almost irresistible.

Emma smiled, looked towards her, and got up from the sofa where, tormented by her emotions, she'd flopped down dead tired just a few minutes ago. How could she possibly refuse? "You're lucky, sweetie. I've still got a few pieces of chicken in the fridge. Otherwise it would have to be scrambled eggs," said Emma, pretending that everything was perfectly normal.

Sara jumped for joy. "Yippee! I love you, Mummy!" she cried, clapping her hands.

Emma rinsed the rice and sprinkled the chicken with spices before putting it in the oven. Her movements were mechanical. Her mind was far away. A thought flickered through her mind: *Is Mr. Bibi interested in me?* She blushed.

Ever since her divorce from Fadi she had not even thought about men. Sara was her only concern. *What a ridiculous idea! Mr. Bibi is a married man. There was nothing untoward about his words. I did my job and he congratulated me. What's wrong with that?*

The morsels of chicken sizzled away quietly in the oven while Emma incorporated the mushrooms into the thick brownish sauce that was simmering on the front burner. Furtively she stuck her finger into the pot to test the seasoning. "I forgot the salt," she said out loud.

Sara came running into the kitchen. "Did you call me, Mummy?"

Emma smiled. "Set the table, sweetie. It'll be dinner time soon."

Without a moment's hesitation Sara got out the placemats, the glasses, and the knives and forks. Emma felt as though she were floating on a cloud. No matter which way she turned, Mr. Bibi's eyes were following her.

44

Louise did not want to heed the faint voice within her warning her not to call Ameur. She preferred to avoid the look of reproach in Lama's eyes. The encounter with Ameur had snapped her awake. Her entire being was alive again after the brutal break that had thrown her into despondency.

Today a curious feeling flooded over her, urging her to forget Ameur's weakness, to forgive his treachery. She would contact him, give him another chance. *Maybe he's changed his mind. Maybe he convinced his mother. If he hasn't, why did he insist I speak to him?* she wondered, in an ultimate attempt to convince herself.

But what was driving Louise to call Ameur was above all the solitude she felt deep inside. Even though relations with her mother had improved and the two women were making every effort to accommodate each other, mistrust and doubt still lingered, a dark cloud ready to burst at any moment. Louise was still afraid to speak to Alice about her beliefs. With Lama she shared friendship, happiness, confidences, jokes, and tears. But Louise was looking for more: the warmth of a glance, the unspoken words whose meaning was conveyed by a smile.

She had finished her prayer. Now, seated on the edge of her bed, she picked up her phone and dialled Ameur's number. Her heart was throbbing. Should she wait for him to answer or simply hang up?

Suddenly Ameur's voice came to her rescue. "*Salaam,* Louise! I saw your number on my screen. I hope you're fine." His voice seemed calm.

Louise had gooseflesh. After a moment of silence she replied, "I'm fine, God be praised. When we met, you asked me to call you. So here I am."

He laughed quietly. "That's just like you. You never forget—"

Louise interrupted. "This time I've decided to forget what you did. I, uh...I mean, how you listened to your mother and dropped me."

There was an embarrassed silence as Ameur fumbled for words. "I didn't drop you, Louise. It was you who got up and walked out and burned all the bridges. I'm always thinking of you."

Louise felt as though her heart was about to burst through her chest. Ameur's words had turned her inside out. "So what about your cousin, the one in Egypt? Aren't you supposed to be marrying her?"

That was the question that had been burning her lips, but Ameur did not answer it.

"I don't want to discuss these matters on the telephone. Why don't we meet some place? I'll be leaving for Hamilton in three weeks. I've been admitted to med school at McMaster University."

"Congratulations. I didn't know," she said, with a tiny tremolo in her voice.

"How about tomorrow afternoon, in the little café just across from the university? Say, at five o'clock?"

It was as though Louise could see Lama shaking her head— her imagination was playing tricks on her! She thought it over for a moment, then said, "Okay, I'll be there, right after work."

She could hear Ameur's steady breathing. She would like to tell him how much he'd made her suffer, how badly he'd deceived her, but she only whispered, "See you soon."

Ameur responded and they hung up.

Louise sat on her bed, the telephone in one hand and a small decorative cushion in the other. Conflicting feelings collided within her: joy and fear, happiness and concern, hope and despair. She felt strong enough to face up to Ameur but still too weak to confront his charm, or to resist it. Should she tell Lama about the meeting? she wondered, and then recalled her friend's words: *Don't trust that guy. He's a mama's boy. Modern enough to have a Canadian girlfriend but not modern enough to marry her.* Those words had been an anesthetic balm on her still-open wounds.

But Ameur had wormed his way back into her life, and she no longer needed Lama. Her heart would guide her. She could trust it.

45

Only a few days were left before Sally and Sam's wedding. It was late August. The days were warm but the nights were cooler now.

Fawzia Hussein was scurrying to and fro like an ant. Everything was organized, everything prepared. The food was cooked and packed into the fridge; the house was spotless and ready to welcome the guests. Ali Hussein had moved the armchairs from the living room to the garage to make more room. For the day of the ceremony he'd rented plastic chairs covered with white fabric, with a large pink knot on the back of each.

Even though Sally was anxious at the prospect of moving on to another stage of her life, she'd managed to decide what had to be purchased. Nothing luxurious or extravagant, but everything they would need to live together as man and wife: sheets for the double bed, china, kitchen utensils, curtains for the windows of their small apartment.

Sam had rented an apartment in a high-rise building not

far from his parents-in-law. It had a bedroom, living room, kitchen, and bath. He'd put some money aside from his summer job and soon he would begin receiving the bursary that would finance his master's program. The couple would be able to live comfortably. Sally's father had insisted on helping them by buying their furniture. At first Sam had refused, but he finally came around.

For her part, Sally had purchased some pretty gowns to wear indoors to please Sam. As she was a little confused about what was permitted to be worn in the house in the presence of her husband, and was too shy to ask her mother, she had gone online to consult the *fatwa* sources. There she'd found the answers to her questions. With relief she'd gone to the nearest shopping centre and bought two nice-looking short dresses, a pair of fitted pants, and several pieces of fine lingerie. She blushed as she tried them on in her room in front of the mirror. She didn't recognize herself. How good she looked in a dress that showed off her slender figure and the gentle curve of her hips. Who would ever recognize her in that revealing and provocative outfit, her the pious girl who never showed a patch of skin? She looked herself over one more time, thought of Sam, smiled, and shrugged. *The sheikh made it very clear—there's nothing wrong with being beautiful for my husband*, she thought as she hung her new clothes in the closet.

She sighed. She missed Sam's messages. They often spoke on the phone and exchanged emails, but the sense of mystery, of being secret allies, that had once surrounded their relationship had slowly dissipated, and she regretted it. She longed for the palpitations, for the powerful emotions that followed each anonymous message. But she was counting on the days after the wedding to reinforce her links with Sam and to rediscover those lost emotions.

Sally opened her closet again and took another look at the red sari she would wear on her wedding day. Her mother had drummed into her that the marriage wouldn't be real unless the bride wore a sari. Sally could not refuse. In any case, she would be in a room full of women. There she could uncover her hair, apply henna to her hands and feet, put on makeup, and wear whatever her mother desired.

It was an elegant garment with highlights embroidered in gold thread that Fawzia had brought back from Pakistan several years ago. She'd hidden it away as a surprise for Sally on the occasion of her wedding. When her daughter decided to take the niqab, Fawzia had feared she would never wear the fine red sari, but Sally was no longer as stubborn and inflexible as she used to be. She stroked the soft, delicate fabric, draped the shawl over her hair, and then put it back on the hanger that held the sari. She was just about to close the closet door when her father called from downstairs.

"Sally, come quickly!" His voice didn't have its usual upbeat tone. Instead, it was full of apprehension and incredulity. Sally rushed from her room and hurried down the stairs, upset that her father had shattered her dreamlike mood.

Ali was in the living room, where the women would gather; the only furniture that remained was the television set and a chair. The voice of the newsreader echoed in the empty room, and the white and pink garlands that her father had hung from the walls tossed back and forth as Sally came bursting in. "It's terrible! Listen!"

Ali was seated in front of the television, wide-eyed. The perpetual smile had disappeared from his face. Irritated, Sally first thought that her father was about to embark on one of his endless monologues about political tensions between India and Pakistan.

"What's going on?" she managed to mutter, feigning curiosity.

"A big police operation today in Ottawa. They arrested a group of young Muslims—they're talking about a terrorist plot."

Sally frowned. She couldn't figure out why her father was so concerned.

As if riveted to his seat, Ali turned towards Sally and said, "I think Sam is one of the people they've arrested."

Her father had to be joking, she thought. And as if Ali had read his daughter's mind, he said, "Sally, it's true, I'm not teasing you. When they showed the young men wearing handcuffs and looking down at the ground, one of them reminded me of Sam, the way he moved. I think he's one of them."

Sally didn't know whether to believe her father or not. She picked up the handset from the small table in the entry hall and dialled Sam's cellphone. His familiar voice caressed her ear: "This is Sam's voice mail. Please leave a message..."

46

"Would you like to marry me, Emma?" Ezz Bibi's voice was flat, as if the words he'd spoken were both simple and futile, as if he hadn't thought through the implications of his question. From behind his round eyeglasses, he scrutinized Emma's face. The hard and distant look of the first days had completely vanished; the cool remoteness of the first few months had given way to growing intensity following the meeting with the Canadian delegation.

Emma's fingers toyed with the handle of a cup of steaming coffee that she hadn't touched yet. She felt as though she were sinking into her chair, as though heavy chains were dragging her down into a subterranean cavern. She feared that someone might have overheard Mr. Bibi, and turned her head to make sure no one happened to be near them. But everything seemed half-asleep in the coffee shop — the Madeleine, decorated in the Parisian style with small round tables with red-checked tablecloths, its refrigerated showcases full of cakes, croissants, cheeses, and cold cuts.

No one was paying any attention to this particular couple's conversation.

It was ten-thirty in the morning on a day when offices and businesses were closed, too early for regular customers. The waiter who'd brought them their coffee and an almond croissant dusted with confectioner's sugar for Emma hardly seemed awake. He took off his glasses and meticulously wiped them with the bottom edge of his T-shirt, totally absorbed in his work.

Emma looked around for her purse. She wanted to reassure herself by holding on to something familiar. So there had been something to her fears and doubts of recent weeks. Ezz was smiling, his expression an open question. She turned away, not wanting to see the sparkle in his eyes.

Emma did not want her gaze to meet his; she felt trapped between the attraction she felt for this man and her disgust at the idea of betraying the woman who had come to her aid. She shivered.

As though he could read her thoughts, he protested vigorously. "There's nothing wrong, Emma. I've been living here in Dubai for years. I'm all alone. Samia is minding our daughters in Canada. Am I to blame if I meet another woman, fall in love, and marry her?" When he spoke of Samia and his family, Ezz turned emotionless, as if he were talking about work.

Emma's hands were shaking. She thought of Sara and their ice-skating excursion to the big rink at Dubai Mall. Emma had rented skates and a protective helmet for Sara, who glided gracefully over the sparkling ice, around and around the rink, waving at her mother.

Sara could amuse herself. "I'll be back in about twenty minutes. I've got a meeting with my boss right here in the mall,"

Emma told her daughter as she left the rinkside. She'd agreed to meet Ezz Bibi in a nearby café.

"There's something I have to tell you. I'd like to see you tomorrow," Ezz had told her the previous night before leaving the office. Emma found his request strange. She felt awkward, certain that Mr. Bibi was hiding something from her. Her first reflex was to refuse, but how could she say no to her boss? How could she not agree to a request that at first glance seemed perfectly innocent?

Now her legs felt so unsteady she could not get up to leave. A couple came in and the waiter shook himself awake and went over to greet them and take their order. The man and woman were speaking French.

Emma's head was spinning, her heart pounding; she had no idea how she should react. She thought back to Tunisia, to her wedding with Fadi. How happy she had been, with her mother by her side and her mind bursting with ideas for their future life. Fadi had held her hand and whispered in her ear: "We'll never part. Never." Then everything had gone up in smoke — happiness, love, friends, work. And now, in Dubai, a second chance was staring Emma in the face. A man desired her, her job fulfilled her — her heart wanted to cry out, loud and clear, her joy at so much happiness, but something was holding her back.

Emma hesitated, looked at Ezz. Without hiding her emotions, she replied, "Mr. Bibi, your question comes as a surprise to me. I came to Dubai to work. I wasn't planning on starting all over again."

Ezz interrupted her. "But why not? Finding love and a career at the same time, what's wrong with that?"

Emma wanted to tell him what was wrong: not only was Mr. Bibi married, he was married to the very woman who had given her that career.

Ezz continued, "Emma, you know very well that in this country life can be difficult for a woman without a husband and with a child to look after. Forget what people will say. I'll take care of everything. I sincerely love you and I want to marry you."

· The blood was pulsing in Emma's veins. She wanted to be swept away by the man's words. For an instant she closed her eyes and saw herself walking hand in hand with Ezz Bibi through a Dubai shopping centre. But something was missing from that happy image: her daughter, Sara.

"Oh my God! I'm so sorry, Mr. Bibi, I have to run. Sara is waiting for me."

"There's no hurry. And please, don't give me your answer before you've thought it over. Take all the time you need."

Emma felt the other couple's gaze come to rest on her. The woman was looking her up and down as she blushed like a little girl. She was sorry she'd agreed to this meeting.

She hurried out of the coffee shop. Her dreams had disappeared and reality had caught up with her. *Me, a second wife, a concubine for Mr. Bibi? A fine way to thank Samia.* She strode through the broad aisles of the shopping centre, ignoring the posters, the advertising, the mannequins dressed in glamorous evening dresses. Soon Emma was lost among the crowds of customers—men, women, and children—that had begun to throng this temple of consumption.

The bright lights of the "gold souk," a succession of luxury boutiques that specialized in jewellery, dazzled her as they sparkled on diamond bracelets and necklaces, precious stones, and watches behind scintillating shop windows. It was as though she'd been swept away to El Dorado, the land where it rained gold dust. She was like a feather blown hither and thither by violent winds, not knowing when it would come to earth.

At last she reached the gateway to the arena. Sara was nowhere to be seen. Her heart beat faster still. In panic her eyes flitted from left to right. She looked closely at the skaters. There was no trace of Sara. *Where's my daughter? O God, do not punish me! I should never have listened to Mr. Bibi's nonsense.* For a brief instant guilt surged through her.

She was about to search the locker room when she saw Sara. There she was seated in the bleachers, rosy-cheeked, fine hair stuck to her sweaty head, a broad smile on her face. "Mummy, how come you're late?"

Emma did not know whether to laugh or cry. Pale, mouth gaping, she had just experienced the fright of her life. She took Sara in her arms and rocked her gently. "Did you have a good time?" she finally managed to articulate.

"Oh, Mummy, it was terrific! Much better than the skating rinks in Ottawa. Bring me here again."

Emma continued to hug Sara and sway from side to side. A bizarre thought flashed through her mind: *Flee. Escape from this place and wipe Mr. Bibi's advances from your memory.*

But where could she go? She did not know. She could already feel Dubai's artificial happiness beginning to fade.

47

Brazilia was the name of a little café not far from the campus. It was like a second home for customers of every description—they came to drink a cup of coffee, sip a chai latte, read a newspaper, or simply enjoy a quiet moment. There were down-and-out students dressed like hippies, with braided hair or shaven heads, discussing their courses, their problems, and life in general. They would chatter noisily and crack jokes as they knocked back their daily dose of caffeine. There were other, less visible students, the quieter ones who always sat at the same tables at the back of the café, finishing a project or simply passing the time of day; their murmuring sounded like the lazy buzzing of bees in a flower garden. The occasional professor or civil servant would drop in, lost in thought, totally detached from the ambient din.

The café walls were painted light maroon and decorated with photographs of Ottawa dating from the early twentieth century. The light fixtures consisted of globes draped with thick multicoloured fabric that hung within a few inches of the round wooden tables. Clustered around each table were chairs in numbers that varied according to the group that chose to sit there. Warm, bewitching music lent the café an exotic feel.

Louise left work at around four-thirty in the afternoon. She had spent the entire day thinking about Ameur. Each time she was tempted to forget about their appointment, something reminded her of it. When she walked through the waiting room on the way to heat up her lunch, she had the feeling that the hands of the clock were watching her closely, as if to say it was only a few hours until they would meet. Later, as she made the day's final round, helping several patients make themselves comfortable in their wheelchairs, the numbers on the digital clock flashed as if to remind her that it was time to leave.

Louise changed out of her uniform and into her street clothes. It was warm, but the early autumn was already showing its colours: the leaves were tipped with red. Louise strode towards her appointment, trying to imagine what Ameur would say. Nervous excitement was getting the better of her — she was smiling at life.

At the back of the café she sat down at a free table, ordered a glass of lemonade, and waited. She took a sip, then put down the glass because it was too sweet. Ameur came in with his customary gait, a blissful smile on his face, eyes cast downward, moving towards her.

"How are you doing?" he asked.

"Fine," answered Louise. "And you?"

Ameur's face darkened. "My mother and I aren't getting along too well these days. I don't want to marry my cousin and Mother is upset. You can cut the atmosphere at home with a knife."

Louise's face lit up. "So why don't you want to marry your cousin?"

Ameur seemed to hesitate, then said, "It's too complicated to bring her here. There are immigration forms to fill out, and then it takes between eight and twelve months before she can come. I just can't wait that long."

Louise was a bit disturbed. She'd hoped that Ameur would tell her that he loved only her, but he seemed in no hurry to say it. There was something else on his mind.

Ameur hated bureaucracy and loved efficiency. Louise was close at hand. He could pluck her right then and there. He caught himself. "And Louise, you know it's you I've wanted from the start."

Louise forgave him his first mistake. He'd just said what she wanted to hear. She let him continue.

"I'll be leaving for Hamilton in three weeks. I'll be looking for an apartment and then starting med school. I want you to come with me. We'll get married and we'll live together, far from all our problems here."

The news burst like a bombshell in Louise's ears. She took another drink of lemonade, forgetting how sweet it was. "What about your mother? Doesn't she count for anything? A little while ago you wanted to obey her whatever the cost and you were determined to end our relationship, and now you're saying all that doesn't matter anymore. I'd like to know what's behind this change of mind of yours. I don't get it."

Louise's counterattack took Ameur by surprise. He did not expect to be challenged; he was so certain that Louise was still blinded by love. "Please, Louise, don't punish me for such a trifle. Over the past months I've been thinking a lot, and my mind is made up. We've got to marry. It's what's best for both of us. What do you say?"

Louise sat there, mouth open wide. Ameur's words rolled over her like a bulldozer. She had hoped he would tell her about his love, his passion, tell her how sorry he was, but he had done nothing of the kind. He'd come with one idea in mind—get married and settle down.

"I have to think it over. I can't just leave my job on a whim. I need some time."

A look of relief suffused Ameur's tense features. "Call me whenever you feel like it. I'll wait for you. In three weeks everything will be fine and our new life will begin."

Louise smiled faintly. Ameur's proposal had left her ill at ease. "I'll call you, it's a pro—Yes, I'll get back to you." She got to her feet.

Ameur said goodbye and watched her leave in silence. Once again his eyes shone. His plan was working perfectly. He couldn't be more satisfied. He was already planning their life together in Hamilton.

48

Ali Hussein was not dreaming, not seeing things. His eyes were not playing tricks on him and he wasn't making it up. The blurred image he'd seen on the television screen had indeed been Sam, his future son-in-law, Sally's fiancé.

It took a long time to convince Sally that The Boy Next Door, the man she loved and who was about to become her husband, was in custody on terrorism charges. The hours that passed were long, and during those interminable hours Sally's life completely changed direction.

Gone were her connections with the religious websites and discussion forums. She spent hours on the telephone seeking an answer to the doubts detonating in her mind. She had not watched television for such a long time, but now she sat riveted in front of the screen, staring again and again at the blurred and shaky videos taken by excited journalists who pursued the accused in an attempt to identify them. She rediscovered her old reflexes, zapping from one channel to another in an effort to understand what had happened, to convince herself that the tall, slender silhouette she was looking at was not Sam. But no matter which channel she switched to, the story was the same. Listening closely, she understood that everything was confused, murky, impossible to confirm; the news coverage was based on hypotheses. The commentators and journalists really knew very little.

The media spectacle, in which fear, sensationalism, and voyeurism had overcome information, was of no help at all to Sally in facing the storm that was sweeping over her. "Is that really Sam?" she kept repeating. "And if it's really him, how did he get mixed up in something like this?" Her convictions were weakening by the minute.

A frigid silence descended over the Hussein household. Fawzia's joyous cassettes went quiet; Ali's contagious laughter came to an abrupt stop; Sally retreated into terrified silence. The only sound to break the deathly stillness was the journalists' voices echoing from the television set.

Sally dialled Sam's number again. Her fingers were trembling. She could feel her knees buckling beneath the weight of her body. Every time she called she hoped she would hear his voice, calm and collected, telling her that everything was all right, that it wasn't his back that she had seen on television, but the only response was the monotone of his voicemail.

"I've got an idea!" Ali Hussein blurted as if awakening from a deep sleep. "Why don't we call the Ottawa police and tell them how wor—"

He didn't finish his sentence. His wife interrupted him, eyes gleaming, mouth quivering. "You're not calling anybody! For the time being we don't know what's going on. Yes, it's true, the pictures look a lot like..." It was as though her mouth could not bring itself to utter the word *Sam*. "...like Sam, but we can't be sure. Maybe it's someone who looks like him. I think the best thing is to wait a little longer, until tonight..."

Sally's gaze swung from her father to her mother, and an immense sadness swept over her. She was moving into uncharted territory; she was a survivor of a shipwreck without a life jacket.

But they would not have to wait until the evening. One of Sam's old friends, whose name Sally recognized from the guest list for the wedding, called. "Hello, my name is Marc. May I speak to Sally, please?"

Questions swirled through Sally's mind like moths seeking light. "It's m-me," she managed to stammer.

"Sally, I've got bad news for you."

Those were precisely the words that Sally feared hearing, words that had haunted her ever since she first saw the images on the television set.

"Sam called a few minutes ago. He's in the Ottawa Detention Centre. He's too upset to call you, so he begged me to do it. He gave me your number. He wants a lawyer."

Sally couldn't bear to hear anything more. Her ears were roaring, the wedding tambourines were pounding. She blurted out, "Thank you for calling, Marc."

"I don't know anything about what's happened. I'm so sorry. But Sam wanted you to hear something else—he says he's innocent. I'm really sorry," Marc repeated. "I'll call again if I have any news. Good luck..."

Sally hung up. Ali and Fawzia rushed over to her.

Her mother was first to speak. "What is it, darling? You look dizzy. Was Sam arrested?"

Sally flung herself into her mother's arms, sobbing like a baby. Ali felt more and more useless. Standing there, hands in his pockets, a look of confusion on his face, he murmured some incomprehensible words.

"Yes, it's him, Mommy. It's him, all right. Sam is in jail."

Sally repeated the same words over and over as Fawzia tried to comfort her.

"There, there, my darling, everything will be fine, *insha'Allah*. I'm sure there's been a terrible mistake. You'll see."

49

Ever since the meeting at the café, Emma's life had taken a new turn. She loathed going to work, pretending that everything was perfectly normal and chatting nonchalantly with her colleagues. She could not face Ezz's admiring gaze. He was still awaiting her response and she did everything to avoid being alone with him.

Every day had become a veritable torment that tore at her skin and ripped it to shreds; every day this torment penetrated her skull like a constant roar. Stretched out in her bed after kissing Sara and turning off the lights, she relived the scene in the Café Madeleine. She recalled Ezz Bibi's mirthful eyes, his imperturbable bearing, his preposterous explanations, that Clark Gable pencil moustache of his. *My Lord, how will I ever get out of here? How will I escape this trap? Poor Samia, if she only knew...*

Emma was trapped. *If I resign without providing a valid reason I'll lose two months' salary and I'll end up penniless in a foreign country. And if I stay, I'll have to live with Ezz Bibi's invasive, piercing stare. How can he imagine marrying a second woman without divorcing the first? It may be legal in this country, but how can he even think of such a thing? Doesn't he care about his daughters, his wife, their friends? Is this his way of taking revenge on Samia for refusing to return to Dubai with him? Is Ezz Bibi using me to humiliate his demanding wife?*

Emma was lost in a labyrinth of fantasy. One moment she imagined herself dropping everything and fleeing with her daughter, never to see this country or Mr. Bibi again, and the next she imagined herself married to him, radiant, forgetting Samia and his daughters in Canada. Worst of all, Emma felt attracted to Ezz. She was drawn to his self-confidence, his courtliness, the insistent way he spoke to her and looked at her.

And as if that wasn't enough, Sara, who adored her new life, had begun to complain about her teacher. The incident had taken place a few days after the marriage proposal. Sara was registered in a private school where her courses were in English, but she also had classes in Arabic and French. She had much more homework than back in Ottawa, but Sara liked to read and to study.

She was finding Arabic difficult. Sara spoke the language but had difficulty reading it, and she could not write long sentences. The Arabic teacher, a very strict Egyptian woman, shouted at her pupils and threatened them if they did not finish their homework. "If you don't do as I say, you will have to copy the same passage one hundred times over!"

Telling the story to Emma, Sara placed her fists on her hips and raised her voice. Then she frowned while shaking her finger at an imaginary classroom, imitating her teacher. "I don't want to go to Arabic lessons anymore. That lady scares me. She's really mean."

Sara sighed when she did her homework. Her handwriting was shaky, but she did everything she could to avoid erasing her letters and having to start all over again. Emma encouraged her to be patient. It wouldn't be long before her marks improved, and then she wouldn't be afraid.

"No, Mummy, that's not it at all. It's not just my marks, it's the teacher who scares me. She's really, really nasty."

Emma laughed in an attempt to calm her daughter. She didn't want things to get blown out of proportion. "Sara, you're exaggerating. You've seen 101 Dalmatians too many times. Your Arabic teacher isn't Cruella. She's just a bit too strict."

But Sara was right, and the situation got worse. One day when Emma picked up Sara after school, she found her daughter with puffy eyes and a red face.

Emma stopped in her tracks. "What happened?"

Embarrassed, Sara did not dare tell her. She whispered, "I'll tell you all about it in the car, Mummy." She shook her head and sniffled as she tried to hold back tears.

"Tell me what happened, sweetie. Did someone hit you? Speak up. I have to know."

Sara did not answer. Her miserable appearance was breaking Emma's heart. Almost running, she took her daughter by the hand and led her to the car. They sat down in the back seat, far from the eyes of passersby. Sara, feeling safer, began to speak.

"It's my Arabic teacher. You didn't believe me when I told you how mean she is. You know what she said to me? I was standing up, taking my books from my bag and getting ready to sit down. Then she began to shout at me from the front of the classroom. 'Hey, you! Yes, you, the fat little cow! Do you think you're a real Canadian? Well, you're not above the law. You sit down right this minute. This isn't Canada, this is the Emirates!'" Sara's trembling voice was interrupted by sobs.

Emma felt like a volcano about to erupt. With one hand she caressed her daughter's face while Sara went on with her story.

"Then she came over to me and grabbed my homework, the assignment I did yesterday with you. She looked at it and then tore it up, right in front of the whole class. Then she yelled, 'Not only won't you do what I say, you're a little good-for-nothing!'" Sara stopped for a moment, unable to speak for sobbing.

Emma felt as if Sara, her happy, joyous little girl, had become lost. Before her sat an unhappy child, choking on her sorrow.

"Sara, look at me, sweetie. Tomorrow I'll have a talk with the principal. The teacher cannot treat you that way. There, there. I promise you it will never happen again." Emma kissed her daughter and then moved to the driver's seat. "We're going home. You're going to have a rest and we'll talk about it again, okay?"

Sara nodded. She seemed to be consoled. All the way home, Emma thought long and hard about the two recent events that had disturbed their honeymoon in this magical city. After the embrace of the first days, it was as if Dubai had shown its claws, had begun to sharpen them and to rip at their flesh.

50

Louise couldn't keep the secret any longer. She was about to burst. She wanted to shout out loud that Ameur had changed his mind, that he was ready to marry her. But she was no longer naive, unlike the first time around. This Louise was still in love but she was bruised, a skeptical Louise, a wiser Louise who had emerged stronger from her first match with Ameur.

True, she had gone to meet him. She still wanted to see his face, to hear his voice, to dream about him. But now she was far less spontaneous, less impulsive, and—most of all—very suspicious. *I'll give him the benefit of the doubt, but I'll be on my guard. I'm not going to get caught in his game another time*, she said to herself as she tried vainly to reach Lama.

Her friend's home line was always busy. Louise expected that Lama would be upset with her because she'd met Ameur again, but she was convinced she'd made the right decision. *How could I have known what he wanted from me, what he wanted to tell me?*

At last the line was free. She heard the childlike voice of Mrs. Bibi. *"Salaam, ya habibi....* You want to speak to Lama? I'll call her." Her voice reverberated in Louise's ear.

"How're you doing?" piped up Lama, a bit short of breath.

"What were you doing?" Louise asked, curious.

"I was watching the news on Al Jazeera. They're rioting in Egypt because the price of bread went up. Everything looks like it's about to fall apart over there."

Louise went on, not missing a beat. The news didn't interest her. "I've been calling you nonstop and the line's always busy."

Lama muttered, "It's Mother. Always the same story, gabbing with some friend of hers. I'm not kidding, she must have been on the phone for more than an hour."

Louise burst out laughing. All Lama could do was criticize her mother and her habits. There was no way she could accept her as she was.

"I've got news for you. I saw Ameur at the Brazilia. He says he's ready to marry me. Do you think his mother will allow him?"

Lama did not respond.

"Hello, Lama! Are you there?"

Lama was in a state of shock. She had worried that Louise might meet with Ameur, but his marriage proposal stunned her. "You can't be serious," she finally managed to sputter.

"Yes, I swear it's true. Listen, Lama, I realize my behaviour upsets you, but put yourself in my place. I wanted to find out why he wanted to see me. It was too much for me."

Lama wanted to show her friend how much she disagreed. "And how do you feel? Are you happy at last, now that he wants to marry you?"

Louise let out a sigh. "Lama, spare the sarcasm. It's not like you. And you know what? I don't feel one bit happier! I don't understand Ameur's sudden change of heart. It's strange. I want to believe him but I have plenty of questions—and most of all, plenty of fears..."

Lama, apparently having found her voice, broke in. "So why don't you ask him those questions?"

"Please, Lama, enough with the snide remarks. Listen to me. I was stuck. I had to see him, had to follow my heart. I felt so alone. I wanted to rub everything out, start all over again. But life isn't a fairy tale, not the way I feel today it isn't. Funny, I thought I'd feel happy, but I feel exactly the opposite. I'm not even sure he's really sincere." With a lump in her throat, Louise paused to take a deep breath.

Lama seized the opportunity to speak up. "Aha, at last! Now you're beginning to grasp what a hypocrite that guy is. Me, I've known he's two-faced for a long time. But you, you're letting your emotions take you for a ride. All you see are his dark eyes, all you hear are his honeyed words..."

Louise tried to defend herself. "You can say whatever you want, I forgive you. I thought his proposal would make me happy, that I'd jump for joy, but nothing of the kind happened. In fact, I'm feeling more hurt than before. Inside I'm bleeding, Lama."

When she heard the pain in her friend's voice, Lama backed off and attempted to smooth things over. "Okay, fine, let's declare a truce. I won't hold it against you that you met him. If we get together on Saturday, we can talk it over some more."

Louise quickly agreed. Their friendship was what counted. Ameur was not going to come between them.

"So, Saturday it is," Lama exclaimed, as if nothing had happened.

By the time she put down the handset, Louise was feeling better. Lama might be hard on her but she was her best friend, and she wasn't about to carry a grudge. Besides, Lama was right to be upset. In her heart she gave thanks to God for placing such a strong friend on her path. The urge to pray swept over her. Without her prayer robe, her head uncovered, she dropped to her knees, forehead touching the floor. "O my Lord, I am so grateful. Protect me from danger and guide me onto the straight path."

For the first time since she'd become a Muslim, the words came to her naturally. No need to remember the complicated formulas Ameur had written down in her notebook. Slowly, surely, his ghost was disappearing.

51

Information about Sam was coming out in dribs and drabs. The media were talking about a major plot: ten young Muslims, all converts, were planning to blow up the House of Commons. The police boasted about the arrests, but the population was divided on the issue. One group believed everything they heard on television or read in the papers. Then there were the skeptics who doubted everything and criticized everything that was said or written. Finally there were the indifferent, who frowned and changed the channel when the reports flashed across their television screens. And Sally and her family were right in the middle of it.

Sally, her eyes red and her face puffed up, was sitting in the kitchen with her parents. Ali, a hangdog look on his face, was like a little boy saddened by the loss of his best friend. Ali had found in Sam the son he never had. He had appreciated his simplicity, the way he looked him in the eye, his frankness. For months now, as he drove his taxi through the streets of Ottawa, Ali had been constructing a dream in which he saw droves of grandchildren, outings in the park, family vacations in Pakistan. Now it had all gone up in smoke. He couldn't tell whether it was the beginning of a nightmare or a light fog soon to be burned away by the sun.

Fawzia had resisted her fatigue from the marriage preparations and the drama that was unfolding before their very eyes as best she could. She was doing everything to support her daughter, to console her, to strengthen her morale. But she also had to call the guests to alert them that, "due to extenuating circumstances," the wedding would be postponed to a later date. At the other end of the line Fawzia heard the ohs and ahs of disappointment, but no one asked too many questions. Nor did she see any need to provide a detailed explanation of the postponement. People would figure it out for themselves soon enough.

Sally was torn between the pain of seeing her fiancé arrested and a powerful wish to find out exactly why. "Mommy, he says he's innocent. I hope so, but what was he doing with that group? It doesn't make sense…" She wept until her cheeks were wet.

Ali had to turn his head away because he could not bear to see his daughter in such a state.

Fawzia said, "In a few days, *insha'Allah*, we'll know why. Your father will speak to a lawyer and you can visit Sam. Be patient, my darling. Every unhappiness will surely end."

But Sally was used to finding answers immediately on the Internet and she couldn't wait. "Who else was arrested? Why didn't he ever tell me about them? And why did those guys want to attack Parliament and kill people?"

Sam had never breathed a word to her about politics, nor

about violence. Sally had always found him peaceful, gentle, balanced. She couldn't recall a single remark, a single comment, anything that Sam might have done in her presence to indicate any violent affiliation or ideology. "And what if Sam is a schemer, someone who leads two lives, who lured me into his trap? What do I really know about him, anyway?"

Sally knew Sam's name and address. She knew that his mother lived in Quebec and that he visited her regularly. In fact, his mother was expected to attend the wedding. Sally also knew that his father lived in Saudi Arabia and Sam had never seen him except in photographs. His father had left Canada, never to return. And she had heard about Marc, his boyhood friend, who worked at a computer company. That was all Sally knew about Sam's circle.

"Gang of young extremist converts...terrorist plot... planned attacks..." Sally felt as though she were playing a bit part in a movie. Who could have imagined that her life would take such a turn? Doubt gnawed away at her. She was beginning to see herself as the victim of an elaborate manipulation instigated by Sam, but then his plea, as reported by Marc, returned to haunt her: *I am innocent.*

Those three words illuminated the darkness that surrounded her. She hung fast to them, like a shipwreck survivor in a storm.

52

Liliane Khoury, the principal of Sara's school, was Lebanese. A woman who carried herself with a certain elegance, she wore her hair short and held her head high, her shoulders curved ever so slightly forward and her glasses pushed up on her forehead to keep her bangs out of her eyes. She was probably in her fifties, but nothing about her betrayed her age as she strolled up and down the corridors, supervising the pupils as they entered their classrooms. Emma had met her when she registered her daughter at the start of the school year. She found the principal to be courteous but a bit chilly. Liliane Khoury spoke impeccable French, rolling her *r*'s and from time to time adding a *yaani* to remind whomever she was with of her Arab identity.

The day after Sara's brush with her Arabic teacher, Emma left the house early to take her to school. She left a message on her office receptionist's voicemail to say that she would be delayed. She avoided speaking directly to Ezz Bibi.

Emma waited patiently in the room just outside the

principal's office. The secretary, still a bit drowsy, offered her coffee. She declined.

"A glass of water, then? Madam Khoury will be here any minute," replied the secretary with a nod. She left the room, rolling her hips.

Emma rehearsed the speech she had prepared the night before. After the bell had rung and the pupils lined up and entered their classrooms, a strange silence settled over the building. Emma could hear the principal's footsteps approaching.

"Madam Emma, how are you?"

The principal was smiling, her voice firm, as she held out her hand. She unlocked the door to her office and showed Emma to a chair. Emma went over the story, taking great pains to repeat the Arabic teacher's exact words. The principal jotted down notes on a pad of paper, a look of concern on her face.

"I am aware that this lady, who is very experienced, can be very strict, but I have difficulty imagining how things could get so far out of hand. I shall look into the matter, I assure you." With these words she ended the meeting and showed Emma, speechless, to the door.

Emma felt that the principal had not taken her story seriously. She suspected that Madam Khoury did not like such complaints, which might damage the reputation of the school and upset its routine. She felt as if she had been dismissed; she felt humiliated and desperate, and more like returning home than putting up with another day of dealing with Ezz Bibi.

Why do you insist on pretending to be one of those courageous heroines who never betray their principles when all around you there's nothing but hypocrisy and deceit? After all, Ezz Bibi is a wealthy man. He's polite, respected by his employees. He really seems to love you. It was that nasal voice again, hissing in Emma's ears. She shook her head to silence it.

As Emma headed for the school parking lot her mind was racing. *This is no place for me. I've got to find a way out as fast as I—*

She stopped in her tracks. A man was standing in front of her car. The silhouette was familiar. She wanted to turn around then and there, but Ezz Bibi had already spotted her. He waved. *What does he want with me now? What's he doing here? How did he know I was at Sara's school?*

Her head was spinning. Mr. Bibi smiled at her. She felt as though she were suffocating, as though she could hardly swallow.

"I was expecting to give you the good news at the office this morning. The receptionist told me you would be late, and I know that you always drive Sara to school." Ezz Bibi was impeccably dressed as usual: suit well pressed, matching tie, hair combed back, moustache nicely trimmed.

Already discouraged, Emma felt as if her knees were about to give way; she began to sway. Ezz Bibi noticed nothing. A hot wind had sprung up, and grains of sand were beginning to fly every which way. She feigned a smile, muttered a greeting, and looked Ezz in the eye.

"Mr. al-Arish has agreed. We will be signing a contract with the Canadians, and you will be promoted to project director. What do you think? Isn't it terrific news?"

Emma did not know whether to laugh or cry. Ezz Bibi was trying to buy her with a promotion! She smiled. "I am very grateful for your confidence, Mr. Bibi—"

He interrupted her. "Ezz. Call me Ezz, if you please."

She pretended not to have heard, and went on. "It's a great honour for me, Ez—Mr. Bibi."

He wanted to stop her but let her continue. Emma kept talking, though she was saying nothing. She had only one aim: to ward off Mr. Bibi's advances and get away as rapidly as she could.

Ezz Bibi let her go on and on, but a single question burned on his lips. "Tell me, Emma, did you think over what I asked you the other day? I always believed I was a patient man, but now I realize I'm not. I'm really anxious to hear what you have to say."

He moved close to Emma. She could feel the touch of his shoulder against hers. Her heart beat faster—physical contact made her feel vulnerable. Her face had turned purple and the flood of words from her mouth dried up. Looking desperately for a way out, she stammered, "Mr. Bibi, you are married, the father of three girls. I know your family in Ottawa. Mrs. Bibi welcomed me into her home and showed confidence in me. I will not bite the hand she held out to me. I cannot accept your proposal. No, I could never do such a thing."

Emma's whole body was shaking but she was relieved to have spoken up. Mr. Bibi stood there, motionless. He'd listened to her without a word, fingering the keys to his car, which was parked next to Emma's. A shroud of sadness slipped across his eyes. Emma thought she saw the spark she'd noticed as they left their meeting with the Canadian delegation slowly fading.

"Is that your final answer?" he asked.

She hesitated. The high-pitched voice inside her whispered:

You're crazy to reject his offer. He really loves you. And you've got to admit it: you're in love with him — your heart beats faster when you see him, you mumble like a teenager. You've got a chance to rebuild your life with a mature man, not someone who's still stuck in adolescence like Fadi, and now you're saying no? You're thinking about Mrs. Bibi, aren't you? Well, too bad for her if she couldn't keep her husband with those extravagant tastes of hers . . .

Suddenly Emma felt like reaching out to take Ezz Bibi's hand, to accept his proposal, but the words were already taking shape in her mouth: "Mr. Bibi, my decision is irrevocable."

He smiled and his face once more assumed its mask of indifference. Then he waved goodbye and got into his car. Emma stood leaning against hers as he drove away. The desert wind was blowing harder and clouds filled the sky. A sandstorm was on the way.

53

Samia Bibi was feeling lower by the day, but her anxiety level was soaring. Ever since her friend Leila had made those insinuations about Ezz and Emma, she couldn't think of anything else. Unable to concentrate on day-to-day life, she spent hours languishing in a dream world.

When she talked to her husband, everything seemed perfectly normal. They chatted about their respective lives and his upcoming visit to Ottawa for the winter holidays. There was nothing to indicate that trouble might be brewing, but still doubt gnawed away at her.

What if I flew to Dubai without telling him? Maybe I'd find out what's really going on, she said to herself, lounging in bed in her pyjamas, her mind wandering, doing everything she could to avoid starting another day full of unanswered questions. But she came to her senses rapidly. *I couldn't leave my three daughters alone at home. What would people say? They would think there's a problem, and it would look like Leila was right after all.*

Curled up in a ball, she lamented her fate. Then, all at once, a wonderful idea occurred to her. *Why don't I throw a party? I'll invite Leila and all our friends, I'll have something else to think about, I'll forget the whole business, and most of all, Leila won't be able to run around saying there's something wrong with me, that poor Samia is upset, that she can only think about her absent husband!* The idea shook her out of her lethargy.

She threw off the covers, jumped out of bed, and strode out of the bedroom. Lynne and Mona's laughter filled the house. The two girls were stretched out, each on a sofa, in the living room, watching a film. Samia turned on the burner to brew herself a cup of Turkish coffee, then picked up the telephone from the kitchen counter. The girls' constant giggling was getting on her nerves, so she called out, "Quiet down, you two! I've got some important calls to make."

She'd left the coffee pot unattended on the stove. Tiny brown bubbles hissed and sputtered on the burner, like tiny rivulets of lava pouring from an erupting volcano as the coffee boiled over. Samia smiled—her mother had often told her that spilled coffee was a good omen. She wiped up the mess, poured what was left into a minuscule cup, took a sip, and began to call her friends.

Samia spent the next two days in the kitchen. She made kibbeh, soaking cracked wheat in water, then mixing it with minced lamb until it formed a smooth paste; she shaped the mixture into elongated balls that she stuffed with pine nuts and fried ground meat and then fried them in hot oil. Other delicacies were not far behind: miniature triangular savouries, each stuffed with spinach, meat, or cheese; grilled eggplant purée; vine leaves stuffed with rice and meat; ground chickpeas seasoned with lemon juice, garlic, and tahini. She threaded chicken and shrimps on skewers for grilling on the backyard barbecue. She ordered sweets from Praline, a Lebanese pastry shop that sold tiny cakes filled with pistachios, toasted almonds, and hazelnuts, in addition to tasty classic French pastries. Samia wanted the best of both worlds — traditional and Arab, Western and Eastern — side by side to give her guests greater choice and to tantalize their taste buds.

She forgot her sadness and the demons and dark thoughts that had been tormenting her. She wanted only to dazzle her guests and to find some peace of mind. And she succeeded — almost.

All the guests had confirmed, all except Leila. Her daughter was sick, and she had no one to look after her. "Dearie, I'm just devastated, but I can't make it. My little one is ill," Leila repeated over the telephone, a malicious edge in her voice.

It was too late for Samia to postpone the party to accommodate her friend. She knew that Leila's slightly indisposed daughter gave her a perfect excuse not to witness Samia's high spirits contradict the rumours she'd been spreading.

SAMIA HAD LEFT nothing to chance. She'd put out jugs of mango and kiwi juice, Thermoses full of tea, pots of coffee. Tables covered with embroidered cloths were piled high with sweets. The ladies filled their plates with food, then sat down either in the dining room or on ottomans placed casually on the garden patio.

Dressed in a Moroccan caftan she'd purchased in Dubai, her hair done up in a chignon with curls that fell about her ears, Samia was in splendid form. She hadn't put on too much makeup—it was all a matter of simplicity of the kind you'd expect from the queen of the party.

"Your mother's a wonder!" Louise whispered to Lama.

Lama shrugged. Her mother's behaviour had ceased to impress her long ago. The two girls were sitting on bamboo chairs in the garden. Candles had been lit to keep the mosquitoes away and provide soft light as night began to fall.

"So, what's next for your lover and future husband?" asked Lama, eyes sparkling mischievously.

Louise jabbed her with an elbow. "Come on, Lama, cut the funny stuff. Who said he was my future husband?"

Lama was wide-eyed. "Don't tell me you've changed your mind again!"

Louise turned serious. "Lama, I've been thinking it over and I think I'm better off without Ameur. I thought I could forgive him. It's true that I rushed off to see him because I thought I would give him a second chance, but I overestimated myself. I'm still too angry with him. I've made up my mind I'm not going to see him again, or even call him."

Lama was startled. She hadn't expected Louise to show such determination concerning Ameur. She said with a smile, "Louise, one of my mother's friends—over there, the one in the yellow dress—thinks you're really cute. She asked Mom if you were married. She'd like to know if you want to become her daughter-in-law." Then she burst out laughing as Louise nearly choked on a half-eaten kibbeh.

Her mouth still full, Louise managed to sputter a few words. "Well, you can tell her quite frankly that I'm not ready just yet..."

54

It was supposed to be the day of Sally and Sam's wedding, but the ceremony had been cancelled. Fawzia and Ali had taken down the garlands. The red sari with the gold embroidery hung from its hanger in Sally's closet alongside her new dresses. The dishes that Fawzia had prepared remained in the fridge. The only occupant of the apartment the young couple had rented was silence. What joy could emanate from it? Ali was considering subletting the place for a few months while they waited to see what would become of Sam.

Sam's name had been made public, along with those of the other members of the group. The media frenzy had begun to subside; the story was no longer making headlines. Only the security experts kept attempting to analyze what could possibly drive young Canadian converts to turn against their own country. Sally spent hours in front of the television, hoping to glean a bit of information or an explanation that would help her understand what had happened. It was a waste of time: she hadn't learned anything new.

Today, she was certain, the meeting with the lawyer her father had hired to represent Sam would help her get a better grasp of the situation. Later, in company with the lawyer, she would visit Sam at the detention centre.

The office of Mr. Ladder, the barrister, was located in one of downtown Ottawa's tallest buildings. He was a criminal lawyer who had helped many people who found themselves in difficult circumstances. Ali had paid a substantial sum to retain his services. He wanted his daughter to be happy. And he wanted Sam to be a free man.

Sally accompanied her father. She wanted to find out exactly what Sam was accused of, to discuss his defence, and to find out if he could be released on bail. She held her breath as the luxurious elevator with its mirrored walls carried them to the seventeenth floor. Her father, standing beside her, forced himself to smile to lessen the tension. Sally felt like weeping.

An elegantly dressed woman received them. "We have an appointment with Mr. Ladder," Ali Hussein said in a low voice.

The woman smiled, picked up the handset, and said in a loud voice, "Your ten o'clock appointment is here, Mr. Ladder." She turned to Sally and her father, smiled again, and asked them to take a seat in the waiting room, where low smoked-glass tables were strewn with magazines.

Sally was determined to keep her mind clear and free. Nothing would distract her. Ali Hussein picked up a newspaper and started to read.

They did not have long to wait. Fifteen minutes later the lawyer appeared, heading towards Sally and her father with a determined stride. He was a tall man whose penetrating gaze shone from behind his round glasses; his curly salt-and-pepper hair lent his face a youthful look despite his fifty-some years. "Come with me, please," he said, stretching out his hand to Mr. Hussein and nodding slightly towards Sally.

He beckoned towards a corridor that lay beyond the wooden door. Sally and her father followed him. The lawyer opened the door to a large room, its floor covered with thick beige carpeting. An oval table occupied the centre of the room and several pieces of abstract art hung on the walls. "Please take a seat."

An uneasy silence followed. Mr. Ladder opened one of the files he carried, glanced at it, and began. "Obviously I am seeing you today to share with you what I have been able to find out about Sam in the course of my telephone conversations and my discussions with the Crown prosecutor. Sam is suspected of belonging to a terrorist cell of young men who were plotting an attack on Parliament. These young men purchased sixty-five fifty-pound sacks of ammonium nitrate to make a bomb and kill people here in Ottawa. Of course, you understand that I am simply summarizing the Crown's allegations. None of this directly implicates Sam, but I must consider all the elements of the government's case and talk with Sam to find out more before moving on to the next step." He cleared his throat, then continued: "Do you have any questions?"

Sally couldn't restrain herself any longer. "But Sam never said a word about any such group or about any plot. He's a student. He was going to start work on his master's in a few weeks. He doesn't have time for that kind of activity!"

The lawyer did not appear to be bothered that a young lady whose face was covered had spoken to him quite so vigorously. "Exactly. That's what I'm trying to figure out, by talking with Sam and closely examining the Crown's case for prosecution. For the time being, we have to convince the judge that Sam can be released on bail until trial."

Ali smiled timidly and asked, "Do you think it's possible the judge will agree?"

"He might, but there's no guarantee. I'm working on it, but we must be prepared for every eventuality. I will need letters of guarantee from people who know Sam, and we will also need a bail fund. I can suggest to the judge that Sam wear a GPS bracelet so that his movements can be traced. In a word, we must leave nothing to chance."

The lawyer's words left Sally feeling ill at ease. She did not like legal jargon, and as a computer specialist, she wanted immediate results. Mr. Ladder glanced at his watch to indicate that he had another appointment.

"Can we visit Sam this afternoon?" Sally asked.

"Oh yes, I almost forgot to tell you. I've obtained an authorization from the detention centre. You will be able to see him from two until three this afternoon. I'll see you then at the centre." He gathered up his files and left the room. As Sally and her father watched him go, Mr. Ladder waved, turned on his heel, and returned to his office.

"Now what do we do?" Sally asked her father.

"We go home. After, we'll go to the detention centre."

"Do you think they'll let Sam go free?" she asked when they were in the elevator.

The question appeared to surprise Ali. "Of course they will! I'm really optimistic. By the grace of God, Sam will be released."

Sally fell silent and under her breath began to recite a prayer. She felt her BlackBerry vibrate in her handbag but she let it ring. As the elevator made its way down, she continued to pray.

55

Emma had never seen anything like it. Powerful, violent winds carrying clouds of sand swept across the city. The fine grains stung the skin like mosquitoes, working their way into eyes, ears, nostrils, and mouth. They put teeth on edge and grounded aircraft, slipped beneath doorways and through cracks in windows and into automobiles; they rushed along like a herd of wild animals, depositing a fine layer of beige that reduced visibility to almost nothing on highways, buildings, and bridges.

Like a strange fog, the sand rattled against the car windows with a high-pitched whine. The sandstorm hit as Emma and Sara were on their way home. Emma could see cars in front of her zigzagging across the highway as though their drivers had lost control, as though they were drunk. She slowed down and began to say a prayer, sitting bolt upright, rigid with fear.

The magic of Dubai, its luxury automobiles, its skyscrapers that gleamed by day and by night, had vanished, hidden by minuscule grains of sand that blew their scorching, putrid breath across the city. In the parks, bushes lurched to and fro in the gusting wind, so violently that they seemed to be shaken by demons of the desert. Only the palm trees, heads held high, resisted the sandstorm. Tall and straight they stood, their fronds dancing in the midst of the whirlwind.

Emma and Sara finally reached their apartment safe and sound. For a while Emma had been afraid they might not make it. A fine layer of sand covered the tables, the kitchen counters, and the floor.

Sara was worried. How would they ever get rid of all that dirt?

"It's only dust, sweetheart. At least we're safe indoors. We'll mop it all up later."

"You know something, Mummy? I like blizzards better than sandstorms. I don't like the taste of crushed glass in my mouth." She laughed and grimaced at the same time to show her disgust.

Emma peered out the window. The wind was subsiding and thunder rumbled across the sky. Sara huddled close to her mother. Soon fat drops were striking the windows with a deafening roar. After the sand and the wind, now driving rain was pouring down on the city. Rushing streams sprang up in the streets, carrying before them plastic bags, cigarette packs, and other refuse. In an instant, broad puddles formed. The city's storm drains, built for an arid climate, were overwhelmed by the sudden onslaught, blocked by a mixture of sand and garbage. Manhole covers popped open, spewing geysers of brownish water.

As Emma contemplated the power of nature she reflected on her own life. For all the hesitation and fears of recent weeks, she felt proud and confident. She had resisted Ezz Bibi's advances and her own doubts. She had feared she would prove weak and vulnerable, but today's encounter had demonstrated that she was much stronger than she thought.

Her and her daughter's dignity were worth more than any promotion. She had not yielded. Just as this burning hot land fought back tooth and nail against the extravagances of wealth to assert its deepest nature, Emma had repulsed Mr. Bibi's egotistical and mindless advances. She had succeeded in tearing herself free from the bewitching curtain of the city that held her prisoner.

Outside, the storm was abating. The heavy rain had become a drizzle. Sara was lying down on the sofa, looking at a comic book.

Emma smiled and sat down beside her. "Sara, today I made a big decision and I want to talk to you about it."

Sara put down the comic. Her eyes were wide, a faint smile on her lips. "Well, are you going to tell me what it is?" she sighed.

Emma fell silent for a moment, searching for the right words. Her eyes shone. "Sara, this country is not for us. I'm resigning. We're going back home to Ottawa."

Sara threw her arms around her mother's neck. "Hooray! That means I won't have to see Cruella anymore! Is it really true, Mummy?"

"Yes, it's true. Tomorrow I'll go and see Mr. Bibi. Then we can go home."

Suddenly Sara was worried. "But Mummy, how will we live back there? You won't have a job."

Emma touched her daughter's hair and caressed it lovingly.

"Don't you worry. We'll get by. I've saved some money, so we'll see what happens."

Now Sara was dancing on the tips of her toes, twirling back and forth. Emma joined her and they held hands like professional dancers. As Sara executed pirouettes, Emma accompanied her, humming her favourite song. Outside, night had fallen. The cars that had sought shelter during the storm reappeared on the streets. From the window their headlights shone like the eyes of a wolf pack in the darkness. Oblivious, Emma and Sara danced on, laughing and singing.

56

Louise came home from the party at Lama's house feeling light-hearted and happy. She had felt quite at home. She knew she could confide in Lama without fear of being judged. Ameur's shadow was fading and she felt alive again. Their last meeting had given her insight. She had really made up her mind not to get involved with him again.

It was completely dark when Louise closed the door furtively behind her. Alice Gendron was watching TV in the living room.

Louise sat down in an armchair beside her mother. "Hi, Mum," she said.

"Hi," Alice replied, almost inaudibly.

At the sight of her mother's drawn features, Louise tried to lighten things up. "I ate too much! My tummy is about to burst!"

Her mother pretended to listen to her, not saying a word.

"Lama's party was great. The weather was just perfect for eating and talking outside. It did me a world of good. I even forgot about Ameur."

Louise had rarely spoken his name in her mother's presence. Now she wanted to see her reaction.

Alice looked at her daughter, startled. "Why are you telling me this? It's your life to live," she exclaimed.

"I know. But I want you to know that I'm not under anybody's influence. Ameur is no longer part of my life."

Louise sensed her mother's satisfaction, but Alice was not letting anything show. Her face was impassive. "Even though that boy is not part of your life anymore, are you still insisting on being a Muslim?"

Louise bit her tongue, let her mother finish her sentence, and then replied, "Mum, yes, I'm a Muslim and I'm going to keep on being a Muslim. It's my spiritual choice and I'm going to live with it. It has nothing to do with my relationship with Ameur. Just because he's left my life doesn't mean I'll change my religion."

Alice closed her eyes. That was her way of showing her disagreement and indicating that she didn't want to hear anything more about it.

Louise would have liked to talk with her, but she realized that her mother was not ready to listen. Alice switched off the television, put the remote on the table, and went to her room.

Louise was alone in the living room. Silence filled the empty space. From far away came the rumble of a bus making its way along the main street. The room was in perfect order, spic and span, not a particle of dust on the knickknacks that lined the shelves. The colourful design of the Persian carpet contrasted brilliantly with the dreary appearance of the other furniture.

Louise contemplated the decor as though she were seeing

it for the first time. She thought about her future. In a few months she would graduate and become a nurse; she would soon be reaching one of her first goals in life. Still, her relationship with Ameur had ended in failure. Life was more complicated than she'd imagined. She'd begun to understand that it did not always conform to one's desires. *For sure I can't have it all—religion, a degree, a husband, and my mother's approval. But I've made up my mind. It may be painful, but I've got to stick to it,* she mused, almost aloud.

Deep fatigue overcame her; it was time for bed. In her bedroom, the prayer mat Ameur had given her caught her eye as it lay folded atop the bed. She no longer wanted even to look at it—too many memories. She picked up the rug and brought it to her face. Then she hugged the finely woven cloth in a final farewell to Ameur and placed it on a shelf in the closet. *Tomorrow I'll go to the Arab convenience store and buy another. Much better that way...*

$$57$$

The detention centre where Sam was being held was located on the outskirts of Ottawa. Sally and her father had an appointment to meet Mr. Ladder right outside the main entrance to the building.

It was Sally's first visit to a prison. She felt her whole body shiver. A tall metal fence surrounded the structure and a handful of cars were parked in the parking lot. Correctional officers stood guard at the entrance and exit. Surveillance cameras were everywhere. Despite the veil that covered her face, Sally felt each of them focusing on her. She felt sick to her stomach and her hands were shaking. She wanted to turn tail and get away from this dark, forbidding place as fast as she could.

Fortunately, Mr. Ladder appeared, and his self-confident bearing reassured her. She walked along beside her father, waiting impatiently for Sam to appear. The two stood aside to allow their lawyer to speak to the officer in charge of visiting permits. Sally saw him pull a document from his black leather briefcase and show it to the officer, who transcribed the information into the computer in front of him, chewing gum all the while. The lawyer turned to Sally and Ali, waiting there silently, flashed a smile, and spoke once again to the officer. Then an expression of relief passed over his face.

He came over to Ali. "The good news is we'll be able to see Sam. The bad news is that we'll only have a few minutes with him. The officer claims that he's received new instructions. For the time being we'll have to seize the occasion to talk with Sam. Later we'll see if we can challenge the instructions."

Sally didn't understand what was taking place in front of her very eyes. Like a robot she obeyed the lawyer's orders, because she no longer had the strength to venture a question. She'd stopped thinking altogether. Ali could sense his daughter's alarm and took her by the hand — how thankful she was for that.

Two corrections officers led Mr. Ladder, Sally, and Ali into a small room. The walls were painted grey. The floor was covered with faded, stain-blotched tiles, and a table and two benches were the only furniture in that cold and soulless place. Sally felt like a visitor from some foreign land. What a contrast with the elegance of the lawyer's office, and what a difference from the cleanliness of all the other places she had visited in Canada! Sam's arrest was revealing a face of her own country that she had never seen before. And she did not feel strong enough to accept what she was seeing.

Sally, her father, and the lawyer sat down on one of the benches. A few moments went by. Sally murmured a prayer because she wanted to reassure herself, but she had no idea how she would react when she saw Sam.

At last he appeared. Two husky guards escorted him into the room in handcuffs. He was hollow-cheeked, his thin face had a look of resignation, and his eyes darted this way and that, as if he were looking for something. A faint ray of hope flickered in them when he saw Sally seated there with her father and the lawyer.

The guards removed Sam's handcuffs and ordered him to sit down on the other bench, then took up positions at the door. For several seconds no one said a word. Sally wiped her tears with a corner of her face veil, in a state of shock. Ali Hussein attempted to smile at Sam. He wanted to be reassuring but his lips were trembling and his smile came out looking like a grimace.

Finally the lawyer broke the silence. "Hello, Sam, I'm your lawyer. We've come to visit you. I hope you're well."

Sam, who until then had kept his eyes lowered to avoid looking at his visitors, raised his head and said in a low voice, "I'm fine, thank you." Then he turned towards Ali and Sally and said, "*Salaam*, Mr. Hussein. *Salaam*, Sally. I am so sorry to have placed you in such a situation. I am really very sorry." He spoke slowly, his head tilted to one side as though he was afraid of forgetting a letter. His deep-set eyes were filled with sorrow.

"No, do not say such things," Ali replied. "All our prayers are with you and I hope everything will turn out for the best."

Sally opened her mouth to speak, but a choking sob stopped her cold. The sight of Sam in such a state stunned her. She remembered the anonymous messages, the sweet words, their telephone conversations, their plans for the future. She couldn't say anything.

Mr. Ladder came to the rescue. "Listen to me carefully, Sam. We don't have enough time to talk today. I'll be back to speak with you at length because I have to know exactly what happened. I'm working on a petition for bail and I'll need all the details."

Sam seemed relieved. "I'm innocent. I never did anything wrong. I only exchanged emails with some people I knew."

Suddenly Sally felt betrayed. Why hadn't Sam spoken to her about the people he knew? Why hadn't he mentioned those conversations? Why hadn't he said anything about those emails?

"I'm ready to tell you everything I know. I have nothing to hide." He spoke in such a low voice that Sally could barely hear him.

Finally she mustered all her courage and said, "Don't be afraid, Sam. We'll get you out of this place. Hold on, and soon you'll be a free man."

Sam smiled and his face lit up. Clearly those were words he'd been hoping to hear. "This may be a test for us. Thank you all for your support—"

He had not quite finished his sentence when one of the guards came over. His loud voice made Sally jump. "Visiting time is over. You must leave immediately."

They handcuffed Sam once again, and his face took on the look of resignation he'd had at the start of the visit. Then he looked over his shoulder and saw Sally wave at him. He smiled. As he left the room, his slight frame was almost totally obscured by the massive bodies of the two guards.

Outside, the lawyer took his leave of Ali and Sally. She was still stunned by the visit. Today was to have been their wedding day.

58

Daddy dearest,

We're off and running! The session is underway. The pace is a lot faster than last year. I don't have any free time—there's nothing but homework and projects to turn in. Lynne and Mona are working really hard this year. What a difference from before! I'm sure Emma has trained them in excellent work habits. And how are you doing? I'm counting the days until you come back. Above all, don't change your mind at the last minute. You'll be here in the middle of winter. What a difference from the smothering heat of Dubai!

Mommy has started doing yoga —her latest discovery. And she's not seeing Leila any more. Good riddance if you ask me. What a relief not to have to listen to her snarky remarks. I suspect she and Mommy had a falling out over something. She's stopped calling and never comes over to the house. Which is just fine by me!

I'm seeing a lot of my new friend Louise. We get along wonderfully. I've been talking to her about the Emirates. She says *she dreams about going there for a visit. Maybe the two of us will go next summer. I don't really want to work there, but I wouldn't say no to a short visit. In fact, I'm becoming more and more Canadian all the time. I feel at home here, I'm making friends, I like my courses, and every day I learn something new about life. Even my arguments with Mommy aren't like they used to be. I've learned to "manage" her, as people say here.*

I'm happy that your project with the Canadians is working out so well. What about your associate? Does he still listen to you? Or does he still insist on doing everything his way, playing it by instinct? Why don't you start a business here? You could use my professional skills, and we'd all be so happy to see you here at home every day. Why don't we talk it over when you're with us next December?

Time to go and get back to my studying. I've got another project to finish.

Hugs and kisses,
Your daughter,

Lama

It was almost nine o'clock at night. Lama was in her room. From the next room came faint noises: her sisters whispering as they did their homework together. Lama shrugged. The two girls were still behaving like kids, totally oblivious to the world around them. *Maybe one day they'll realize that they've grown up and that they won't be Mommy's little darlings indefinitely.* Lama sighed, rubbed her eyes as if to eradicate the slightest urge to sleep, and then sat down in front of the computer.

In her room at the end of the hall, Samia Bibi lay face down on her green yoga mat. Her short legs were stretched out behind her and her head lay lightly on the mat. Unblinking, her eyes were focused on a point. Her slightly fleshy arms were spread out, each thrown to one side. Samia breathed deeply, trying not to forget the instructions Angela, her yoga instructor, had given her. She lay motionless for a moment and then raised her legs behind her head, her arms forming a V, her chest compressed by the weight of her stomach. She felt herself as light as a feather, as if she were about to take flight. This was the best position for eliminating bad thoughts.

Jealousy had just about thrown her into depression. Luckily she'd chanced upon an ad for yoga lessons being given in the neighbourhood, and it had changed her life. It was love at first sight. The yoga positions helped her focus on her body, listen to her breathing, and not be obsessed with doubt. Around the same time, Samia had stopped seeing Leila. There were no more morning get-togethers over Turkish coffee; but now she had something else to satisfy her. Her only remaining weakness was shopping.

But evening gowns and elegant ensembles no longer interested her. No, it was clear she had enough. Now she only had eyes for sportswear such as yoga tanks, special tops to restrain her breasts and display her navel, and pretty bands that kept her hair in place. Samia bought all the new outfits, because she couldn't get enough. They made her feel young and beautiful, the way she'd felt when she lived in Kuwait and dreamed of the Prince Charming who would rescue her, who would carry her away from that living hell.

59

Emma could hardly believe what was happening. In a few minutes she would be seeing her mother again, after so many years of absence.

It had all happened so fast. A week earlier she had resigned her position in Mr. Bibi's company and made up her mind to return to Canada. It had taken her a few months to sort out her feelings. Dubai was a mirage in the middle of the desert and a mousetrap for the vulnerable. But Emma was not prepared to take a bite of that tempting cheese in exchange for her dignity and her principles. It was true that she felt a powerful attraction for Ezz Bibi, and perhaps she had just missed the chance to start her life all over again. But at what price? Never could she have forgiven herself for betraying Samia, who had been so generous to her. Never could she have agreed to play second fiddle in the strange relationship between Ezz and his first wife.

Sara was happy about leaving. She didn't want to be humiliated in front of her classmates anymore. Emma knew the Arabic teacher would not change her attitude, and enrolling Sara in another private school would only postpone the problem.

In the middle of the night a telephone call had awakened Emma. "Emma, it's me, Aunt Zohra, your mother's sister. Can you hear me?" asked the voice of an elderly woman.

"Auntie Zohra! How are you?" Emma's heart was beating as if it would burst. Something terrible must have happened; otherwise Auntie Zohra would not be calling her at such a late hour. She thought of her mother. *O God, let her be alive,* she prayed.

Auntie Zohra coughed, then said, "Everything is fine, just fine, my little one. Your mother is a bit sick. She's got a nasty case of the flu. When I went to visit her yesterday, she whispered in my ear, 'I really miss Emma. I'm afraid I'll die before I see her again.' At first I didn't want to mention it to you because I didn't want to upset you. You know, when you get old, you think a lot about death. I haven't been able to get my sister's words out of my mind, so I decided to let you know."

Emma's eyes flooded with tears. The call made her forget her own worries. How well she remembered Auntie Zohra, who always had on hand a box of *halva chamia* — "Damascus-style halva," they called it in Tunis. It was made of ground sesame seeds and sugar. Auntie Zohra would pass it around to all the young nieces and nephews who came calling. Emma adored that halva, which was cut into small bites that disintegrated as soon as you touched them. She liked it best spread with butter on a slice of bread. Emma could still taste its sweetness.

"Auntie Zohra, tell me the truth! Is my mother really sick?"

The elderly lady seemed to hesitate, then stammered, "Not at all, my little one. Don't you worry your head. But you know something? I think it would be best for you if you came to see her."

"*Insha'Allah*, Auntie Zohra, I'll do everything I can."

The call went on for just a few moments more before the elderly woman hung up, not wanting to disturb her niece any longer.

Emma could not get back to sleep. Auntie Zohra's attitude had been ambiguous. She suspected that her aunt was hiding her mother's true condition from her. If not, why all the talk about death? Emma knew that people of her mother's generation never spoke of death directly, but she had gotten her aunt's message: *Your mother is gravely ill. Come to her bedside as fast as you can.*

Emma's official reason for resigning was to care for her sick mother. Ezz Bibi's reaction was cool and businesslike. He handed Emma her last paycheque and thanked her with no display of emotion. "I wish you all the best...Emma." He had hesitated before pronouncing her name, but forced himself to do so.

Emma looked straight at him. Ezz Bibi knew how to control his emotions. He remained stone-faced. "Thank you, Mr. Bibi, for your understanding, and for giving me the opportunity to work with you."

Ezz Bibi opened his mouth, but then he turned and walked out of Emma's office, leaving her speechless and sad.

EMMA'S TAXI PULLED up in front of her family home. Sara was close beside her. It was a small house, located in Ariana, an inner suburb of Tunis. Long ago it had been the country's rose capital. In the springtime you could smell their perfume as you strolled down its narrow lanes. But the bitter stench of passing cars and trucks had replaced all of that.

The garden was not as well-kept as when her father was still alive. The white paint had begun to peel and the garden gate was rusty. The shutters were closed. Her childhood home looked abandoned, a house of ghosts. Emma's heart sank, and she was overcome with guilt. *Why did I let so many years go by without coming back? How could I let my mother live alone in this house? The telephone calls were not enough, that's clear. I should have come much sooner,* she thought.

Emma pushed open the garden gate with her foot and set her luggage down on the ceramic-paved path. Sara was wide-eyed, half curious and half surprised by the place.

Emma shivered. She'd forgotten how the damp cold of Tunis could pierce you to the bone. No one knew she was coming. Even Auntie Zohra had no idea. The night before, when she had called her mother to find out how she was doing, she hadn't breathed a word. "How are you, Mum?" Emma had asked.

"God be praised, I'm fine. I always pray for you and your daughter."

Emma knew that her mother would never ask her to come home just for her. She would have been too reluctant to interrupt her daughter's career.

She came to a stop in front of the blue door. The laughter of her childhood surged up from her memory. She saw herself happy, watching an old comedy on television with her parents. Emma's hand was shaking as her finger pushed the doorbell.

The few fruit trees in the yard, denuded and contorted by the cold, oscillated like the hands of an ancient clock.

Then the blue door opened and an old woman appeared. Her face was wrinkled, her back bent. Was Emma hallucinating? Was this really her mother? It was only her benevolent gaze that Emma recognized. How frail she had become!

Emma could not contain her emotion. Everything came surging to the surface: Fadi, the divorce, poverty, Dubai, Ezz Bibi's strange proposition... The river overflowed its banks and its rushing waters flooded the lowlands. She threw herself into her mother's arms.

Sara looked on in silence. A scrawny cat with a motley coat made its way across the road, mewing noisily. No one noticed it go by.

GLOSSARY

Shahada: the testament that all Muslims must utter in order to adopt their new faith.

The *Night of Power,* which occurs during the month of Ramadan, is sacred to Muslims. Many believe that one's wishes will be granted on that night.

Fatwa: a ruling in response to questions of daily life or any other subject, usually issued by a religious authority such as a sheikh or an imam.

Ulema: a generic term used to describe Islamic scholars; singular: *alim*.

Insha'Allah: God willing.

Mabruk: Congratulations

Habibi: "dearest," a staple expression in Arab popular music.

"Yaani:" "that is," an expression frequently used in several dialects of Arabic.

MONIA MAZIGH was born and raised in Tunisia and immigrated to Canada in 1991. Mazigh was catapulted onto the public stage in 2002 when her husband, Maher Arar, was deported to Syria, where he was tortured and held without charge. She campaigned tirelessly for his release. Mazigh holds a Ph.D. in finance from McGill University. She has published a memoir, *Hope and Despair,* her account of her successful struggle to free her husband. Her novel, *Miroirs et mirages,* was published in the original French in 2011 and was a finalist for the Trillium Book Award.

International journalist and award-winning literary translator FRED A. REED is also a respected specialist on politics and religion in the Middle East. He has reported extensively on Middle Eastern affairs for *La Presse*, CBC Radio-Canada, and *Le Devoir*. A three-time winner of the Governor General's Literary Award for Translation, Reed has translated many works, including Monia Mazigh's memoir *Hope and Despair*, with Patricia Claxon. Fred A. Reed lives in Montreal.